IN MEMORY
OF
DONNA ROBERTS

Methuselah's Heart

Methuselah's Heart

Sequel to
Methuselah's Gift

Mary Elizabeth Edgren

ILLUSTRATED BY
KATHRYN PENK KOCH

THOMAS NELSON PUBLISHERS
Nashville • Atlanta • London • Vancouver

Published in Nashville, Tennessee, by Thomas Nelson, Inc., Publishers, and
distributed in Canada by Word Communications, Ltd., Richmond, British
Columbia, and in the United Kingdom by Word (UK), Ltd., Milton Keynes,
England.

Scripture quotations are from:

The NEW KING JAMES VERSION of the Bible. Copyright © 1979, 1980, 1982,
1990, Thomas Nelson, Inc., Publishers.

The HOLY BIBLE, NEW INTERNATIONAL VERSION®. Copyright © 1973,
1978, 1984 by International Bible Society. Used by permission of Zondervan Bible
Publishing House. All rights reserved.

The "NIV" and "New International Version" trademarks are registered in the United
States Patent and Trademark Office by International Bible Society. Use of either
trademark requires the permission of International Bible Society.

The NEW REVISED STANDARD VERSION of the Bible © 1989 by the Division
of Christian Education of the National Council of the Churches of Christ in the
U.S.A. All rights reserved.

THE NEW AMERICAN STANDARD BIBLE, Copyright © 1960, 1962, 1963,
1968, 1971, 1972, 1973, 1975, 1977 by The Lockman Foundation and are used by
permission.

The Holy Bible, KING JAMES VERSION.

Library of Congress Cataloging-in-Publication Data

Edgren, Mary Elizabeth.
    Methuselah's heart / Mary Elizabeth Edgren : illustrated by Kathryn Penk Koch.
      p. cm.
    Sequel to : Methuselah's gift.
    ISBN 0-7852-7962-8 (hc)
    1. Raccoons—Fiction. I. Title.
PS3555.D478M49 1995
813'.54—dc20   95–14509
                                                                  CIP

Printed in the United States of America
1 2 3 4 5 6 7 — 01 00 99 98 97 96 95

To
All my grandchildren

Contents

$\mathcal{N}$ote from
the Author

How wonderful it is to see our "furry friends" again—some direct descendants, I am sure, of our past visitors. Each one is unique, with his or her own special set of characteristics. Yet there is an amazing resemblance to the characters in my story, including a real live Waddler without a tail. This cannot be just a coincidence.

Each day as we watch this new generation of "furry friends," we are reminded of our own family. How quickly the years have gone, and now Trasher and Puddly have families of their own. By the time this story is published, Posie will also be married. Except for the cycle repeating itself, this would be a sad time for us. But it is not. We are already enjoying the new generation— three precious grandchildren—and we look forward to even more. It won't be long before we'll have them all on our laps reading to them about our "furry friends." But for now, they are still trying to master the word *raccoon*.

I am grateful also to my husband Jim, my beloved partner of thirty-three years, for his faithful support and endless help in reading, rereading, and editing the manuscript.

Finally, my special thanks to Sheryl R. Taylor and Lonnie Hull DuPont, as well as many others at Thomas Nelson for all they have done. We have shared a wonderful relationship and the whole experience has been one which I will always treasure.

Mary Elizabeth Edgren
Lakewood, Washington
1995

CHAPTER 1

Remembrance

He cares for you.
1 Peter 5:7

OVER IN the farthest corner of the tree house, away from all the rest, lay a curled-up heap of fur, and from it came a sniffle, a little whine now and then, and finally a moan. Posie was crying. It wasn't that she was hungry or even cold, though the winter had come upon them in all its fury. It was that, deep in her heart, she had an ache that would not go away, and it was best described as a "Grandfather ache." Methuselah was gone. And it didn't seem to matter what she did or where she went—the ache was always there.

She tried to tell herself that she was older now (and on the outside she *had* grown up quite a bit), but deep down inside she felt like a little raccoon again, and she wondered if she would ever stop hurting. Though she desperately wanted to live for The Maker, she found that the continual ache in her heart kept her from thinking of anything or anyone else—including The Maker.

Slowly, she lifted her head, and as she did, her dried wreath slid down over one eye. It was the last wreath her grandfather had helped her make, and she did not want to lose it. She took it off and fingered it tenderly. Oh, how she wished that she had something more from her grandfather than a dried wreath! If only he had left something else. Then maybe the ache in her heart would go away, and then she would be able to serve The Maker again.

Methuselah

She looked around her. Aunt Serenity was sleeping peacefully, but now and then she sighed—a deep, sad sigh. Her parents, Seeker and Tidy-Paw, were closest to her, and they, too, moaned from time to time. Trasher and Puddly, her older brothers, were curled up in the other corner, and next to them, Waddler, their newly adopted member. She listened intently for any sounds coming from them. There were no sounds, but they tossed and turned fitfully in their sleep. Last of all, she watched Furry-Ball and Sunshine, her little brothers. They whined and cried as if they were having very bad dreams.

Yes, the others were hurting too! Posie realized that she wasn't alone. But what would become of them without Methuselah, and how could they go on?

Methuselah—they could never forget him. Though he was gone from their lives, he was very much alive in their thoughts and hearts. Perhaps the cruel winter had something to do with it. A howling, icy wind penetrated their drafty tree home, reminding them all the more of their great loss. In fact, there was never a day when they didn't shed tears or share memories about their beloved Methuselah. And sometimes his memory was so alive in their hearts that they actually forgot that he was gone.

Once, Furry-Ball came to breakfast late and blamed it on the fact that he had not heard Methuselah's morning whistle. Then, remembering that Methuselah was gone, he began to sob.

Another time Posie came running into the clearing with some greens that had fallen nearby, yelling, "Grandfather! Grandfather! Look what I found for my wreath!" Then tears filled her eyes as she stammered, "Oh, I forgot. He's not here anymore."

Even Seeker, while translating The Book one day, pointed to a word and asked, "Grandfather, what do you think about . . . ," and then, realizing that it was only Trasher who sat next to him, he wept unashamedly.

Each one grieved in his own way, and yet they also grieved together. They even visited Methuselah's grave, with the hope that it would bring them comfort. But after several trips, they all agreed that it didn't help. Methuselah seemed no closer, and they still could not get over their loss. Nor did they try to at first. But as Posie lay curled up in her corner most of that long, hard winter, how she wished the ache would go away. Eventually, it was their stomachs that reminded them that life had to go on, and they could no longer ignore that hunger.

Furry-Ball put into words what they were all feeling. "I'm *awfully* hungry!" he said. "Why don't we go see if Sarah left any apples for us on the stone wall?"

"Leave it to Furry to think of food. But it would do us all good to have a nice meal," Seeker said with a chuckle. "Now that you mention it, I'm hungry too!" And with that, he sent the youngest raccoons off to look for the apples.

A warm wind had melted the last of the snow, and spring was just around the corner. They had to admit that they felt better being out in the sunlight. Frost sparkled like diamonds wherever the sun shone through, and soon they were skipping along merrily, totally distracted from their grief by the loveliness of what they saw around them in the forest.

Before they knew it, they were at the stone wall. And just as Furry-Ball had predicted, there were the apples. Sarah had placed them in a neat row on top of the wall.

"A letter!" shouted Puddly, the first to see it. Quickly setting the apples down, the others gathered around Puddly as he attempted to read it. "I am . . . ," he translated slowly.

"Sorry!" interjected Posie, pushing her face as close as she could to the letter.

"Methuselah . . . ," continued Puddly.

"Died!" added Trasher.

Putting the words together, Puddly read, "I am sorry Methuselah died." Then translating the next sentence, they were all able to read, "I loved him too. Your Friend, Sarah S."

Tears filled their eyes, and they became very quiet. Posie heaved a deep sigh. "We're not the only ones who are sad. Just think how sad Sarah must feel! I saw her cry when she found Grandfather. And yet, even though she feels sad, she thought of us."

"These apples are proof of that," agreed Trasher.

"And so is this letter," added Puddly. Suddenly, he felt very ashamed. Hanging his head, he said, "We've been thinking only about ourselves."

"If we could just think of a way to cheer *her* up," sighed Posie, and she began to fold the letter.

But as she did so, Sunshine noticed something. "Wait! There's more at the bottom of the letter. What does this mean?" He pointed to some very tiny words that didn't seem to spell anything.

"We'll have to ask Father," they decided, and started for home. As they walked, they realized that once again they had been reminded of Methuselah's death. But this time they felt strangely cheered to think that their friend Sarah, despite her own sadness, cared about them.

As soon as they reached home, Trasher and Seeker immediately set to work translating the tiny words at the bottom of the letter, while Tidy-Paw and Aunt Serenity prepared the apples for their supper that night. And for the first time, they all sat down to eat with joy in their hearts—a joy that was hard to explain. Nothing had changed. Methuselah was still gone. And yet *everything* seemed changed.

Posie tried to express what they all felt. "It helps to know that someone cares when you're sad. I hope we can tell her that we care about her sadness too."

"And she's not the only one who cares," announced Trasher.

"What do you mean, Trash?" asked Puddly.

"Father and I discovered the mystery to those tiny words at the bottom of Sarah's letter. They are code words to help find something very quickly in The Book—and we found it!"

"What does it say?" asked Furry-Ball eagerly.

"It says, 'Cast all your care upon Him, for He cares for you.'"

"Who's *He,* Father . . . ? The Maker? . . . The Maker cares for us?" asked Posie excitedly.

"That He does," Seeker assured her.

"I'm *so* glad Sarah gave us His message," said Posie. "To think that The Maker cares about us!" They thought about that as they settled down, and they all slept better than they had in many a night.

CHAPTER 2

A
New Dawn

*Even in darkness light dawns
for the Upright.*
Psalm 112:4

WAKE UP, everyone, it's spring!" Furry-Ball and Sunshine shouted one bright morning, and so it was! The forest was alive with birds singing and insects buzzing in great swarms. Soft breezes gently lifted the green-sleeved arms of the Douglas firs, displaying delicate new fern tips uncurling beneath them. It was a morning to get out of bed and celebrate! And without so much as even a murmur, they stiffly, but joyfully left the darkness of their winter home and stood in the golden sunlight, savoring the warmth and smell as if it had been their very first experience of spring.

Of course it was not the first for any of them, but it certainly felt like it as they stepped out into the sunlight. "I can't remember the sun ever shining so warmly or the forest ever smelling so good," remarked Waddler. Even Aunt Serenity, who had seen many a spring, agreed. But they didn't seem to know why they felt as they did.

They gathered around the table with a sense of awe and quiet joy, and gave thanks to The Maker for bringing them through the long winter. Then, hungrily, they ate the food that Furry and Sunshine had found earlier that morning.

"It's time for The Book," announced Seeker when they had finished their breakfast. He handed it to Waddler, whose shocked expression betrayed a lack of confidence in his ability to translate. "Just try, Son, and you'll catch on in no time. With lots of practice translating, it'll almost seem like reading."

Waddler began slowly. "The . . . generation . . . of . . . the Upright . . . will . . . be . . . blessed," he read, with many pauses between words.

"But what does that mean?" questioned Sunshine. His thirst for answers was increasing. "Does it mean that only Uprights can be blessed?"

"No, Sunshine," answered Seeker. "It means that we, too, will be blessed if we're Upright in heart. And it means that Grandfather has left us a wonderful example. He was Upright in heart, you see, and now by following his example, we can all be Upright in heart too. By believing in The Maker just as Grandfather did, we, too, will be blessed."

"What does 'blessed' mean?" asked Furry-Ball, not to be outdone by his brother.

Waddler spoke up. "I think it means that The Maker shines on our lives just like the sunshine is shining on us now, warming us and giving us light." He read on, "Even . . . in . . . darkness . . . light . . . dawns . . . for . . . the . . . Upright."

"That's it!" interrupted Posie. "That's what's happened to

us!" She was so excited about her discovery that she could hardly get the words out. "Don't you see it?" She looked at the confusion on their faces. "Just as we stepped out from the darkness into the sunshine this morning, and we felt so excited and warm, that's what happened to our hearts when we believed in The Maker!"

Seeker nodded in agreement and continued. "And not only did we feel the darkness of not believing, that is, until Grandfather's example made us all want to be Upright in heart, but we also have gone through another kind of darkness—the darkness of Grandfather's death."

Waddler added, "And yet, for some reason, I feel such hope—like dawn in the darkness." Once again that sense of quiet awe filled their hearts—until Seeker broke the silence.

Bowing his head, he spoke to The Maker, "Thank You, Dear Maker, for bringing us dawn in our darkness." And his words echoed the thoughts of each of their hearts. It was as if a great fog had cleared away in their minds and they were free to go about the daily business of living once again—yet with a greater determination than they had ever known.

To begin with, Trasher volunteered to lead a food expedition. The rest of the raccoon children gathered around excitedly to hear his directions. But as they scampered off, Waddler turned back momentarily. He approached Seeker respectfully and asked, "If I were to be very careful, could I take The Book with me? I could do some more translating on the trip. You see, it takes me longer than the rest of you, but I think with practice I could get faster."

"Of course, Son," responded Seeker, "as long as you don't get faster than the rest of us!" He smiled and handed him The Book. Waddler held The Book reverently for a moment and then turned to catch up with the others.

When enough food had been gathered and stored, Trasher suggested that they stop and rest. That gave Posie a chance to weave her first spring wreath, and discovering a patch of yellow wood violets, she started her task excitedly. Furry-Ball and Sunshine, still full of energy, began to wrestle and throw cones back and forth. But Waddler drew apart from all the activity and sat down to translate from The Book.

Soon Trasher and Puddly joined him. "We'll help, Wad," they offered. Painstakingly, with only a little help from them, Waddler worked through the document and at last read his translation. A lively discussion followed, and soon, curiosity getting the better of them, the rest were drawn in.

"What does it say, Waddler?" Sunshine asked eagerly.

"It says that The Maker does good to those who are Upright in heart," he answered, a note of sadness in his voice.

"What's wrong with that?" questioned Furry-Ball.

"Nothing's wrong with that, Furry," he replied. "*We're* the ones who are wrong. You see, if The Maker does good to Uprights, we need to do the same, and we aren't doing good to an Upright in heart—our own Upright, Sarah."

"You're right, Wad. We haven't done anything to cheer her up," he admitted.

"But what *can* we do?" Posie put her wreath down and leaned forward.

"I think we ought to let her know that we follow The Maker. That would cheer her up," suggested Puddly.

Furry-Ball's face lit up. "If we went into the Big House and sat down next to her, then she'd know."

"That wouldn't be wise, Furry," Trasher said gently. "Don't you remember how the other Uprights chased you out the last time?"

"You're right. They weren't at all friendly," he admitted. How well Furry-Ball remembered his close call! If it hadn't been for Sarah's help, there was no telling what those Uprights would have done to him.

"Well, it's time to finish up our work," said Trasher, moving off in the direction of the stone wall. Furry-Ball and Sunshine ran on ahead, while the others followed, still discussing ways to cheer up their friend Sarah. They had just come within sight of the wall when suddenly they saw Furry-Ball and Sunshine running back toward them.

Furry-Ball motioned for them to be quiet. Whispering, he said, "She's there—Sarah, I mean. And those others who don't move—they're there too. It's not like before when we had tea. This time they're all sitting in rows and seem to be listening to her."

"She's reading to them from The Book," explained Sunshine. "But it doesn't sound like our language at all."

"Since there are no other Uprights around, couldn't we go and sit there too?" pleaded Furry-Ball. "That would show her that we follow The Maker, and I think it would really cheer her up!"

Trasher was weighing the decision carefully in his mind when Waddler spoke up. "It would be doing good to an Upright in heart, Trash, just as The Maker does."

"You're right, Wad, and so are you, Furry," said Trasher, his mind made up. "It *would* do good to cheer her up. Okay. Everyone follow me!"

It would be impossible to describe Sarah's reaction upon

seeing five raccoons climbing over the wall and taking their places alongside her dolls. But by the time they had settled themselves and looked up, all that they saw was a delighted smile beaming from Sarah's face, and they knew they had accomplished their mission. They had cheered up their little Upright. The darkness of Methuselah's death had passed.

CHAPTER 3

*R*eaching Out

Whoso walketh Uprightly shall be saved.
Proverbs 28:18

IT WAS awfully hard sitting that long," Furry-Ball was saying later to the rest of the family when they had returned from their mission, "but we *had* to cheer her up."

"I thought it would never be over," agreed Sunshine. "I sure wish we could understand her language."

"Well, even though we didn't understand what she said," admitted Posie, "we watched what she did, and we learned a lot. And now we know just what to do to have a Gathering!"

"Do you mean we're going to have to go through this again?" Sunshine looked panic-stricken.

"No need to worry, Son," chuckled Seeker. "I'm sure you cheered her up for a long time to come!"

"Maybe it would be good for us to go through this again, though," Waddler suggested gently.

"I'm not sure what you mean, Son," Seeker said in a puzzled voice.

"Well, Father, maybe it would be good for us to have our own Gathering just like the Uprights—in our own language, of course."

Seeker looked thoughtful for a moment. "We have been gathering each morning to read The Book, but perhaps we need to do more than that. It certainly wouldn't hurt us!" he said with a smile.

"You're right, Father," exclaimed Posie. "It seemed to help

12

so much, and it was *so* interesting! Our Upright made some of those lovely sounds we heard before in the Big House, and she passed around a shell woven with straw and put silver circles in it. Then she talked from The Book. After that, she shook each of our paws and waved, and when she gave that signal, we knew it was time to go. It was *so* wonderful, Father! But . . . if only we understood what all of those things meant."

"We could go to the Big House and look through the clear stone," Trasher suggested, "and find out what the Uprights do at their Gatherings, although we already do know quite a lot. But if we watched carefully, maybe we could find out why they do the things they do and what they all mean."

"I'll go with you, Trash!" Puddly's face lit up. "It would be dangerous, but if we went at night, we could see them and they couldn't see us."

"And when we understand what they do," added Waddler, "we might even be able to think of a better way to do it."

"A better way?" Posie looked surprised.

"Well, we *are* different in some ways," Waddler reminded her, "even though we have Upright hearts. By *better* I mean that maybe we can do some of the things they do in our own way. Just like we read—well, actually we translate—The Book in our own language. Of course, we'll do some things the same—like inviting friends who don't follow The Maker. They do that, you know."

No one spoke. The full meaning of what Waddler had just said suddenly hit them.

Seeker looked up. "Grandfather would have certainly agreed with you, Son. But more important, The Maker does. Why, just this morning I came across the saying, 'Whoso walketh Uprightly shall be saved.' If the opposite is true, unless we give our enemies a chance to know The Maker and become Upright, they're lost. Yes, Son, you're right. We need to have a Gathering in our own language so that we can invite both enemies and friends. We can't keep The Book to ourselves."

"I'm so glad you feel that way, Father," replied Waddler, "because I've been wanting to go back and bring the rest of my family here. I'm sure they'll want to follow The Maker once they hear what's in The Book."

Now at this point, something in Waddler's words jarred his memory. The Book! He had left it behind. In an instant, he pictured just where he had left it—under a fir tree. He would have to go back for it, and the sooner, the better. He would wait for the right moment to slip away unnoticed.

"You have my blessing, Son," Seeker was saying, "to return for your family."

Waddler's thoughts came back to the present, and he thanked Seeker. Then he saw his chance. Without an explanation, Waddler excused himself and set off to find The Book he had so carelessly left behind. Hardly noticing his departure, the family continued their conversation.

"But, Father, where will we gather?" asked Posie. "It would be too hard to build something as beautiful as the Big House."

"We didn't gather in the Big House today," Furry-Ball reminded her. "I don't see what's wrong with gathering outside like our Upright does."

"It wouldn't work, Furry," said Trasher gently. "It wouldn't be safe out in the open on the ground. And Posie's right too. We could never build anything like the Big House."

Aunt Serenity, who had been quiet up to now, spoke, "The Maker will provide. Of that you can be sure." Those words caught their attention. It was as if Methuselah himself had spoken to them. And in a sense he had—at least his words were echoed by Aunt Serenity. Everyone smiled—a smile of realization! The Maker *would* provide! They started making plans immediately with the expectation that they would find a suitable place to gather.

Seeker assigned tasks. "Trasher and Puddly, you'll need to get your sleep during the day so as to be rested enough at night for the trip to the Big House. If we're going to have our own Gathering, we've got to study the Upright Gathering. Posie, you, Furry-Ball, and Sunshine are to gather food. We'll be needing more when Waddler's family comes. And in your travels, be looking for a place suitable for our Gathering."

No sooner had Seeker finished speaking about him than Waddler returned from his secret mission.

"It's gone! The Book is gone!" he announced flatly. He waited for their reaction. There was absolute silence. No one knew what to say. Hanging his head in shame, he said in a shaky voice, "It's all my fault. I should never have taken The Book in the first place."

He looked at them with such a pitiful expression that still no one dared to speak, though each felt in his heart the same sense of loss. "And how can we go on without The Book?" he asked. He was heartbroken, and his grief was obvious.

At last Posie spoke up. "If you are to blame yourself, Waddler, you'll have to include us as well. We were all there too. We *all* left The Book behind." As soon as she said those comforting words, the others joined in, and together they tried to console Waddler in his grief. And yet the ache remained. How could they live without their most precious possession?

For a while they seemed more discouraged than ever. How could they even think of having a Gathering without The Book? Then, out of their despair came a spark of hope. And once again, it came from Aunt Serenity. "The Maker will provide," she said simply.

In the end, Waddler left to bring back his family, but he was no longer discouraged. He had hope that The Maker would provide a place for them to meet and that somehow He would help them find The Book—or provide another.

Their plan to reach out to their enemies had begun to take shape, and now they knew that Aunt Serenity's words echoed what Methuselah had taught them so long ago—The Maker *would* provide.

CHAPTER 4

The *U*pright Tree

Sing, all you who are Upright in heart!
Psalm 32:11

A WEEK HAD passed, and every day the family repeated their chores—finding more food and studying the Upright Gatherings. At the same time, they searched every nook and cranny of the forest for their beloved Book. But their efforts were in vain. It had completely disappeared. And the worst of it was that they feared someone had stolen it—but who?

Despite this, a feeling of excitement filled the air as they returned from their trips. Sometimes they brought interesting reports about the Upright Gatherings, while other times they shared exciting possibilities for their own gathering place.

"Today we saw Uprights put silver circles and green leaves in golden shells." Puddly was describing what they had seen. "We think they were giving gifts to The Maker, but He never came. They just left the shells there."

The next day Puddly could hardly wait to tell the good news. "He came all right. The shells were empty when we got there."

Posie, Furry-Ball, and Sunshine didn't have as much to share, but they were bursting with excitement nonetheless as they explored the area for a gathering place.

Then one day, while picking berries, Posie looked up to see a very tall Douglas fir tree—one that seemed to tower above the others. She sent Furry-Ball up to look around. "Maybe from up there you can see a good place, Furry."

Furry-Ball climbed to the top. He had never been so high. "I can see *everything,*" he exclaimed, "even the Big House!"

"But do you see a place to gather, Furry?" she asked.

"Well, on the way up I did pass a hollow opening right here in this tree. It's quite big inside," he announced. Posie and Sunshine scurried up to see for themselves, and what they saw filled them with excitement. They hurried down to tell the others.

It was late that afternoon when they returned to find the others just getting up. Tidy-Paw and Aunt Serenity had prepared a delicious meal, and they were all so hungry that at first they didn't talk. Then Seeker spoke up.

"We saw Rabid last night. He was with the others, but he didn't seem to be part of them. We talked with him alone and invited him to the Gathering. We told him that the meeting would be at the next full moon and that we'd send him word as to where we'd meet. Now, if only we had a safe gathering place . . ."

"We found a very good tree today, Father," said Posie, remembering what they had seen. "It's quite hollow inside and very big."

"Which one is that?" he asked, straining to picture the one they were describing.

"You know, Father," Furry-Ball reminded him, "it's the one that you can see wherever you are." Seeker still looked perplexed. "It's the most Upright one in the whole forest," Furry-Ball explained emphatically.

Seeker smiled. "Well, if it's the most Upright tree in the forest, Son, that settles it! That's where our Gathering will be!" He smiled again and then laughed. Soon they were all laughing. "Let's go see our new gathering place!" he concluded.

And so they did. When they saw it, they were convinced that The Maker had indeed provided (as Methuselah would have said) a wonderful gathering place—and an Upright one at that!

CHAPTER 5

𝒯allen Hopes

Upright are Your judgments.
Psalm 119:137

CRASH! IT WAS late at night when a clap of thunder woke them all from a sound sleep. And then before they could get resettled, another clap, and still another. It was going to be a storm through which they could not sleep.

"Father, it sounds so close," whispered Furry-Ball in a very frightened voice as he snuggled up to Seeker.

"It is, Son," Seeker assured him, "but The Maker's even closer." He patted Furry-Ball's head tenderly.

Lightning flashed, and in that split second, they saw something terrifying—giant trees swaying back and forth, much farther than they had ever seen them sway. Then once more came a loud crash. Sunshine and Furry-Ball covered their ears.

Again and again lightning streaked across the sky, followed by angry claps of thunder. Closer and closer the storm moved until it seemed to be aiming at the very tree in which they huddled. Great gusts of wind tore through the opening, threatening to pick them up like twigs and blow them away. Holding on to one another, they shook with fear.

"The Maker's here with us," came Seeker's calm voice.

"Indeed He is," Aunt Serenity assured them.

Those words had such a calming effect on the rest of them that when the loudest thunder of all hit, they hardly flinched. And while the trees still swayed frighteningly, each face reflected an inner peace and calm. They had traded their fear for belief in The Maker's protection. Rain came down in sheets, penetrating their once dry hollow home. Huge broken branches went sailing by, and yet somehow they felt safe and waited patiently for the storm to subside. It did at last, but not before a sickening crash told them a great giant of the forest had fallen.

"I wonder which one it was, Father." Puddly whispered anxiously.

"We'll see in the morning, Son," he answered. Then he closed his eyes.

The others did, too, and soon they were all sleeping peacefully, aware of The Maker's protection.

Morning came, but there was nothing about it to remind them of the awful events of the night before. There was no wind, no rain, and the only sounds that greeted them as they awoke were the songs of birds. In fact, they had the feeling that it had all been a terrible nightmare—that is, until they looked out. The forest floor below was strewn with broken branches. Here and there trees were snapped in half as if an angry monster had raged through the forest. The raccoon children looked out in disbelief— never had they seen their forest home in such disarray.

"We've got our work cut out for us," remarked Tidy-Paw. She had noticed that even their table was buried under branches fallen from above.

The family had a makeshift breakfast that morning of food from Aunt Serenity's emergency closet. Then, not having The Book to read, they quoted all that they could from memory. How they wished they had memorized more! Afterward, while the debris was being cleaned up, Seeker led a scouting mission. They had to find out which giant had fallen.

Furry-Ball, running ahead, saw it first. "I knew it!" he sobbed. Then turning from the fallen tree, he raced back with the news.

"It was! I knew it!" was all he could say, and he sobbed even harder.

In spite of all their questions, Furry-Ball could not stop sobbing. He simply could not talk about it.

*There it was—it was not just any giant that had fallen—
it was their Upright Tree.*

Posie sensed this at last and said gently, "Furry-Ball if you can't tell us, show us." He turned, still sobbing, and they followed him to the clearing.

What they saw brought tears to their eyes also. There it was—it was not just *any* giant that had fallen—it was *their* Upright Tree. Its trunk had broken off at the hollow section where it was most rotten, leaving a huge jagged piece still standing. Down below, the remainder of the tree leaned against the tall stump and then stretched out along the ground for almost a hundred feet.

They were totally shaken as they stood there. It was beginning to dawn on them what this would mean. No words could express their disappointment. Then Posie spoke, and her words had a bitter ring to them.

"Why did this have to happen to us? We were almost finished getting it ready for the Gathering, and now we don't have any place to meet at all."

"Then what will we do?" added Puddly. "The full moon will be very soon."

"I guess The Maker didn't provide after all," said Furry-Ball, echoing Posie's bitterness.

Seeker looked at Furry-Ball sternly. "Son," he began, "I don't understand why The Maker didn't protect our Upright Tree either, but we know He's always right, even when it doesn't seem so to us."

No one argued with him, but no one spoke out in agreement either. Instead, they went home and told the others the bad news. Now, no one seemed to have any interest in working. They sat and looked off into space with vacant stares. They just didn't care anymore.

After a long time, Seeker uncovered the notes he had copied laboriously from The Book onto a piece of bark. He began to read quietly to himself.

A few minutes later, he broke the silence. "I thought so," he said. The others looked up, with questions in their eyes. "It says right here that His laws are just."

"Whose laws, Father?" asked Trasher.

"Why, The Maker's, Son."

"What does it mean, Father?" Puddly wanted to know.

"It means that whether The Maker protects or whether He doesn't, He's fair. 'Just' means fair and Upright!"

"Does that mean that He was fair even when He didn't protect our Upright Tree?" asked Furry-Ball.

"That it does, Son," Seeker answered.

"How can that be?" asked Sunshine in disbelief.

"We don't always understand The Maker's ways, Son, but we do know that The Maker is good, and this says that His ways are too."

They went to bed that night not quite convinced of this truth, but no one dared to argue about it with Seeker. And during the next few days, though they looked for a new gathering place, their hearts were just not in it. No one wanted to say the words, but they were deeply disappointed in The Maker and even blamed Him for the loss of their tree. Yet they went through the motions of looking for a new place.

It was on one of these trips that Furry-Ball, Posie, and Sunshine got caught in a sudden thunderstorm. They were very close to the clearing where their giant Upright Tree had fallen.

"Let's hide under the fallen Upright Tree," suggested Furry-Ball. "Its branches are so thick that we won't get wet at all."

Quickly, they scooted under a large branch. For a moment they couldn't see. But when their eyes adjusted to the dim light, they found themselves in a large room with the huge tree trunk for a ceiling and the arched branches forming the walls. (They had never seen a great cathedral, but that was exactly what it looked like inside.) It was rather cozy and completely dry, and they enjoyed their stay immensely. And when at last the sun came out, they knew it instantly. Sunbeams filtered in through the branches as if there were windows spaced evenly along the walls. The effect was quite enchanting, and they hated to leave. They would have to come back again. Reluctantly, they turned to go. But Posie stopped in her tracks.

"That's it!" she exclaimed. The others stopped, too, but looked at her in bewilderment. She just smiled. "You know, even though The Maker didn't protect our Upright Tree, He gave us something much better." Furry-Ball and Sunshine still looked puzzled. "He gave us a fallen tree! It's so much bigger for our Gathering, and it's also very safe."

Furry-Ball was the first to see it. "You're right, Posie! It *is* bigger and much better! Let's go home and tell the others!"

They did, and Seeker didn't seem at all surprised. After returning to see it for themselves, they all agreed (and felt that Methuselah would have too) that The Maker *had* provided a gathering place for them even better than the first one! The Maker's laws *were* just.

Sunbeams filtered in through the branches as if there were windows spaced evenly along the walls.

CHAPTER 6

The Welcome

For the Upright will dwell in the land.
Proverbs 2:21

THEY'RE COMING! They're coming!" Sunshine shouted excitedly from the top of a tall tree. The full moon was just two days away, and Waddler had promised to return in time for the Gathering. Sunshine and Furry-Ball had been looking for Waddler's return for several days, and now at last Waddler and his family were coming. Sunshine slid down the tree in reckless abandon, shouting to Furry-Ball who waited at the bottom. "At last they're here!" To Sunshine's dismay, Furry-Ball did not look at all happy. "What's wrong, Furry? Aren't you glad they're coming?" His voice had a note of concern.

"It's not that, Sunshine. Of course I'm glad. It's just that . . . well . . . we haven't found The Book, and Waddler will be so disappointed." The two walked back toward the clearing in silence, until Sunshine thought of a solution.

"We just won't tell him," he said. "Maybe he'll forget all about The Book."

"Forget about The Book? How could anyone forget about The Book?" Furry-Ball challenged. "No, he won't forget, but we won't hurt his feelings by reminding him. We do have to tell the truth if he asks, though." They both agreed, and reaching the clearing, they announced Waddler's arrival to the others.

Everyone flew into action. Tidy-Paw and Aunt Serenity

quickly prepared food while Posie set shells out on the table. Furry-Ball and Sunshine volunteered to get water, hoping that in the process they would be the first to encounter the approaching visitors. Trasher and Seeker called for Puddly to help them drag a very long log over to the table to seat the newcomers.

And then at last the moment arrived. Waddler stepped into the clearing, his face beaming with joy.

"Welcome back, Son!" said Seeker with outstretched paws as he strode over to greet him. But before Seeker could embrace him, the younger raccoons dashed ahead and all but smothered Waddler with their hugs.

Catching his breath, Waddler said, "It's good to be back! I can't wait to introduce you to my family!" He motioned toward the forest where two figures shyly made their way out of the shadows. The first raccoon stepped into the light. He was the larger and looked quite a bit like Waddler. The second, somewhat smaller, and about the size of Posie, joined him.

At the sight of them, Sunshine and Furry-Ball forgot their manners and, rushing toward the newcomers, nearly knocked them

Faith

over in their excitement. "This is my brother," Sunshine said proudly, before Waddler could even get the words out.

"Welcome!" came a warm greeting from all of them at once.

"And this is our sister," Waddler said, encouraging her to step forward out of the shadows. She was very shy, but her smile was enchantingly lovely. The family, especially Sunshine and Furry-Ball, welcomed her warmly.

After an exchange of greetings, introductions, and other niceties, they all gathered around the table to share their first meal together. Soon conversation flowed so freely that it seemed to them that they had always been a family. Waddler recounted his adventures and then described to them what was to him the highlight of his trip.

"You may be wondering about my family's names," he began. "On our way here, I mean, home," he corrected himself, "my brother told me that I was very different from the brother he once knew." He looked a little embarrassed as he explained. "I told him that it was because I now follow The Maker."

"It's true," his brother broke into the conversation. "And even though I'm older, I asked him to help me do the same. You see, I wanted to be changed too. And now thanks to Waddler, I no longer wear a mask on my heart. I belong to The Maker. I guess that's why Waddler gave me a new name, Truster, because I now trust The Maker."

Waddler turned to his sister. "And sometimes even little sisters choose to follow The Maker," he hinted broadly.

She looked up at him shyly. "I, too, saw a difference in Waddler," she began nervously, "and I knew that I needed to have my heart changed by The Maker. And yet it seemed hard to give up my old ways. You see, I have always been quite nervous and afraid. But because of Waddler's example, I have decided to follow The Maker. And already I feel new inside!" She looked up at them with new courage in her eyes. "I guess Waddler saw the difference, and so he calls me Faith!"

"Now our family is much bigger!" Sunshine boasted excitedly.

"Yes, and that means you will have to *share*, Sunshine!" reminded Waddler.

Truster

Sunshine's face fell, then almost as quickly, it brightened. "Well, it'll be worth it, because pretty soon there'll be more of us who follow The Maker than those bandits! And then maybe there won't be any more badness!"

Waddler smiled, and looking at Sunshine and Furry-Ball, he said, "As long as you two share, there won't be!"

Everyone else laughed and passed shells heaped with food to the guests. When they all had eaten, Waddler said, "Isn't it about time to catch up on what's happened here?"

Furry-Ball and Sunshine seized the opportunity. Carefully avoiding any mention of The Book, they steered the conversation around to the discovery of the fallen Upright Tree. "We can show it to you tomorrow," they offered.

"And what about The Book?" asked Waddler.

Sunshine shot Furry-Ball a warning glance.

"Well, it hasn't turned up yet, Waddler, but we're still looking." Furry-Ball tried to sound encouraging.

Waddler's face fell. "I must confess I'm a little disappointed," he admitted. "But it sounds like The Maker has provided a place to gather. I believe He'll help us get The Book back too."

Sunshine and Furry-Ball were relieved to hear him say that, and soon the conversation turned to more cheerful topics. They chattered well into the night until weariness overtook them.

When at last they went to bed, it was with the realization that what had begun in the heart of Methuselah had now spread to others.

CHAPTER 7

The  Gathering

Let all the Upright in heart praise him!
Psalm 64:10

POSIE RUBBED the sleep out of her eyes. It was the next morning, and she felt like she had barely slept. But noises outside told her that someone was already up. It was Faith, and she was setting the table with shells. They greeted each other shyly, but soon were working together happily. Posie showed her where everything was, and then they hurried to the brook to wash their food. When they got back, they found the rest of the family gathered around the table discussing the Upright Tree.

"The space is a lot bigger now, and it's very safe," Puddly was saying.

"We didn't even get wet when we hid there during a thunderstorm," added Furry-Ball.

"I'm anxious to see it," said Waddler. "Why don't we all go?"

With that, they quickly ate breakfast and set out, Furry-Ball leading the way. Soon they came to the spot, and when they stepped into the clearing, Waddler's mouth fell open in surprise.

"It *is* bigger, Puddly, and it couldn't be safer!" exclaimed Waddler as they inspected the Upright Tree. "It's just as Father said. The Maker's laws *are* good! It'll hold so many more of us than when it was standing. Let's go inside and see it."

They entered the enclosure, and once inside, they were immediately aware of a sweet fragrance. Posie, Furry-Ball, and Sunshine had covered the floor with fir needles, and a soft breeze had spread their scent. Golden sunshine filtered through the side openings, giving them just enough light to see. The effect was enchanting, and for a moment they stood there in silence. Then gradually, in hushed voices, they began to talk about the fallen Upright Tree and how it was just right for them. After listing its many advantages, they all agreed that it *was* The Maker's choice for them.

But Waddler noticed something the others had missed. Standing in front of the huge broken-off stump outside, he said, "This looks just like the pointer on top of the Big House."

"Pointer?" Trasher repeated, puzzled. "I know what you mean on top of the Big House—but why do you call it a pointer?"

"Because it points to The Maker, Trasher. The Uprights always put these on top of their Big Houses. Maybe this will help the bandits know where to come—the pointer will tell them!"

"You're right, Waddler!" exclaimed Puddly. "The Maker planned for everything! And just in time too. Tomorrow is the full moon."

That was all the reminder they needed to hear. They raced for home to begin preparations for their first Gathering. Hoping for a big crowd, they began by sending out invitations to all the bandits. Next, they prepared large amounts of refreshments to be served after the Gathering. At last it was all done, and they went to bed tired, but filled with anticipation.

The next morning, light had hardly dawned when the family was already up and carrying food to the Upright Tree. At last all was in place, with the exception of The Book. They could not help feeling disappointed about that, yet somehow they hoped that The Maker might still answer their prayers. Meanwhile, they wrote down all that they could remember from their translation of The Book, and it was surprising how much they could recall. Then Waddler rang the silver shell that they had hung on the pointer the day before. (Since it was made from an old can, it had a slightly "tinny" sound. You and I would have noticed the difference immediately, but they thought it sounded just like the bell in the Big House.) He had told them that often Uprights used this method to call other Uprights to their Gatherings. A bit skeptical, the others waited down below to watch for the bandits.

"Here they come!" whispered Puddly at last. Loud voices and cracking branches signaled the bandits' arrival, and every eye strained to see them.

Needlenose stepped into the clearing first. He was mangy and scarred, and behind him came a band of outlaws just like him. "So this is your *Upright* Tree!" he snarled mockingly.

"Maybe it was once!" another sneered. "Doesn't look very Upright to me now!"

Raucous laughter followed, and they all turned to leave. All, that is, except Rabid. He stepped forward, and as he did so, they noticed he was carrying something. And then they all saw it at once—it was The Book!

"I've come to the Gathering," he said quietly, his eyes lowered. "I want to return this." He pointed to The Book. "You see, ever since . . . ," he paused for a moment, "ever since Methuselah died for me, I've felt the need to find The Maker. It must have been The Maker who made him do it—no one ever cared whether I lived or died before. I know I'm not good in my heart, but I can learn—if it's not too late." He looked up with a pleading expression.

Seeker smiled and welcomed him warmly. "It's not too late," he said encouragingly. Then, gathering around him, they all went inside.

But when Rabid came out, something was different about him. Oh, he looked the same on the outside, but on the inside he was changed. For the first time, Rabid really understood the true meaning of Methuselah's gift. It was more than just his *life* that had been saved. Methuselah had given him the gift of knowing The Maker, and now this gift was his at last. And as for the others, they had received a gift, too—their beloved Book had been returned. The Maker had heard their prayers.

CHAPTER 8

The
New Follower

My shield is God Most High, who saves
the Upright in heart.
Psalm 7:10

THE SUN turned tiny drops of dew into diamonds hanging from the tip of each leaf, but Puddly never saw them. His head hung down, he kicked stones angrily, and he was muttering under his breath.

"Why do I always get the worst jobs? Father and Waddler get to finish the translation for the next Gathering, and Trasher and Truster get to build the chairs for the Upright Tree, and I'd even rather be helping the girls gather food than do this job."

He climbed a little hill and sat down on a moss-covered log by the side of the path. Almost a month had passed since their first Gathering. "Why can't Rabid come without a special invitation? Doesn't he know how to tell time? I'm sure Father told him clearly. He must know it's the full moon."

He stared down the long, smooth path as if hoping somehow to see Rabid emerge from the shadows, but Rabid did not come. Puddly looked down and continued muttering.

"And besides, don't they know how dangerous it is to be so near enemy territory?" His words sounded vaguely familiar, and he strained to recall another time when he had felt this way. He bent down to kick at a stone, but as he did so, the entire log moved, and before he knew it, he rolled off onto the ground. Stunned for a moment, he struggled to remember the other time when he had felt his job was unimportant. Then as if a light went on in his mind, he recalled the time that they had gone for The Code. Hadn't he felt the same way? And hadn't he learned from that experience that every member's job was important?

He sighed. Yes, he would do his job even if it didn't seem important. Picking himself up, he sat down on the log again. But as he did so, the log moved forward, dumping him once more onto the ground. Distracted from his thoughts, he looked at the log suspiciously. The ground seemed level. What was making the log move? He tugged at the moss and vines covering the base of the log. His paws felt something—something round and hard. Working quickly, he pulled the vines aside to reveal an amazing discovery—something as round as his ball. But there was still more! This ball was different. It was flat and round at the same time, and it was attached to something hard. He worked excitedly to free more of this object, and getting his face as close as he possibly could, he peered through the dark hole in the moss to see not just one round flat ball, but three more! And then he looked upward. The flat balls were attached, all right, to something hard and smooth—but it was definitely not a log. His paws worked feverishly now. He had to find out what this object was!

As he pulled away more and more of the vines and the object became visible, Puddly was sure that he had never seen anything so wonderful before. And just when his curiosity was at its peak, the strange object rolled out, almost running right over Puddly. It was long, oval, and smooth, and it sat on four round, but flat-sided balls. Though still covered with moss on the top, there was no mistaking the handiwork. Uprights had made it. But what was it for?

Puddly eyed it carefully, yet with excitement. And then, as if it were a dangerous animal he was trying to ride, he jumped on its back in one daring leap. To Puddly, at that moment, it must have seemed like a very dangerous animal, because the force of his jump caused the object to move forward with alarming speed. In fact, it would have rolled right down the hill had not an old rotten tree stump been in its path. Once again, Puddly was dumped unceremoniously on the ground. But as he lay there, looking at the moss-covered object, no longer did he wonder about its use. He looked up toward heaven and, smiling, spoke aloud, "Thank You, Dear Maker, for the Upright-mover."

No sooner had he gotten up to push the Upright-mover away from the stump than he heard a groan coming from the

direction of the path. A bent-over figure came into view. It was Rabid, and he was hobbling.

"Rabid!" yelled Puddly in alarm. "What's wrong?"

"Help me," Rabid answered weakly. "I'm hurt." He was bleeding and looked like he was about to collapse.

Puddly rushed to his side and supported him. Half carrying, half dragging him, he managed to get him over to the side of the path. Then very carefully, he leaned him against the Upright-mover.

And when at last he got his breath, Rabid told his story. "They called me a fool," he said in a voice barely audible. "I told them that I now follow The Maker, and I tried to get them to follow Him too. But they wouldn't listen. After a while, they turned on me and chased me out—with rocks. I don't think I've seen the end of them. They're comin' for me. I heard them say they plan to make an end of me." Rabid looked up with fear in his eyes.

Puddly bent down to look at his wounds. "Don't worry, Rabid. They won't come this far. I'll get you home somehow. You'll be safe."

Barely had he spoken those words, however, when a large rock crashed through the branches, landing just inches from Rabid.

Another rock hit and then another and another. Puddly looked up just in time to see a rock land right near the Upright-mover.

"I guess we're not so safe after all," Puddly admitted.

"They're almost here!" Rabid shouted. "It's no use. Just leave me here to die. Save yourself. Don't worry. I know The Maker. I'm not afraid now."

"No, Rabid, I can't," Puddly said flatly. Then one of the bandits came out of the shadows and hurled a rock, hitting the Upright-mover. The rock bounced off, striking Puddly's chest. Partly from pain and partly from determination, Puddly flew into action. "Scoot up onto this log," he ordered Rabid, dragging him up onto the Upright-mover. Rabid made a final effort and pulled himself up, though he did not understand Puddly's strategy. Then, as he heard the bandits closing in on them, Puddly gave the Upright-mover one great push and jumped on.

But it was too late. The bandits were blocking the pathway right where the Upright-mover was headed. Puddly was sure they would be stopped, but a strange thing happened. Because the path was very smooth and slightly sloped at this point, the Upright-mover gained surprising momentum. Puddly had just enough time to see the hateful looks on the faces of his enemies turn to absolute terror as the Upright-mover bore down on them. In fact, Puddly and Rabid were moving at such speed that the bandits barely had enough time to scramble to the side of the path before the Upright-mover hurtled past them. Neither Puddly nor Rabid looked back. But had they done so, this is what they would have seen: their enemies had been stopped dead in their tracks at this strange sight. At least for a moment. Much more quickly than they had come, they left, falling all over themselves in their haste to escape from this terrifying monster.

Meanwhile, Puddly and Rabid literally flew through the air at some points as the mover raced down the hill. Puddly's mind was totally clear, and he found that he could steer the mover when he leaned to the left or the right. At last, reaching a level area, the mover came to a stop. It was absolutely still. Listening carefully and hearing no noise, either from rocks or bandits, they looked at each other in relief and sighed.

"We're safe!" whispered Puddly, still not daring to speak in a normal tone.

"Thanks to The Maker!" answered Rabid.

Then, using a vine still attached to the Upright-mover, Puddly pulled it, with Rabid aboard, along the trail to his new home. But when they got there, to his dismay, no one greeted them. Instead, the family stood speechless as they stared at this strange vehicle.

Puddly broke the spell. "Isn't anyone going to help Rabid? He's hurt!"

Posie and Aunt Serenity moved quickly, tending to Rabid's wounds, while Faith and Tidy-Paw brought him water. The rest gathered around to examine the Upright-mover, amazed at Puddly's story of their escape.

Many days went by. Not only did Rabid heal quickly, but the others felt he learned to translate The Book quickly too. Furry-Ball made a suggestion. "Let's call him Rapid!" he said with a smile. "After all, he sure left those bandits pretty rapidly!" (And that was how Rapid got his new name!)

And as for Puddly, he wondered if Methuselah wouldn't have said that teamwork was getting to be a habit with him!

CHAPTER 9

$\mathcal{D}$edication

An Upright man gives thought to his ways.
Proverbs 21:29

ZOOM! CRASH! The whole family looked up just in time to see Furry-Ball and Sunshine hurtling through the air. The mover on which they were riding had hit a log in their path. Although they had been out practicing their steering, they had not mastered the art at high speeds. They picked themselves up, dusted themselves off, and were back on the mover just in time to hear Seeker's response to their accident.

"Glad you're not hurt, boys, but I think you should be more careful. By that, I mean slow down a bit. After all, it's not every day we find something as valuable as this mover."

Puddly piped up, "Father's right, Furry and Sunshine." He tried not to look too annoyed, but he did feel a certain attachment to his find. "It *is* quite valuable," he continued. "Remember, if it had not been for the mover, Rapid and I would not have made it home safely."

Looking ashamed, Furry-Ball and Sunshine hung their heads and slowly got off the mover.

"It's not all your fault," said Waddler, looking up from his translation work. He put a loving arm around each of them and then faced the questioning looks of the others. "You see, Rapid and I have just been translating an important truth from The Book."

Rapid spoke up. "It says plain and clear, 'An Upright man gives thought to his ways.'" He pointed to The Book. "Couldn't be plainer."

"But we're not 'men' Uprights. We're raccoons," said Furry-Ball.

"True, but I think it means us too," replied Waddler. "After all, we are Upright in heart."

Tidy-Paw looked at Waddler and shook her head in confusion. "Certainly seems to me that's exactly what Furry and Sunshine did *not* do—they gave no thought to their ways." The two chastened raccoons again hung their heads in shame.

"But we never told them it was wrong," replied Waddler. "We never told them that the mover was valuable and that it came from The Maker."

Furry-Ball and Sunshine looked up hopefully, and this time the rest of the family hung their heads.

Seeker spoke up. "You're right, Waddler. Even though Puddly found the mover, it was The Maker who gave it to us, and just in time too. But we didn't appreciate it well enough to protect it. We just took it for granted and let the boys play with it as if it were a toy. We gave them no rules. Why, it's a miracle they haven't wrecked it by now."

No one spoke for a while, and then Furry-Ball broke the silence. "So it's not our fault, right?"

Everyone laughed. Everyone, that is, except Furry-Ball and Sunshine. They looked more confused than ever.

"Well, whose fault is it then?" Sunshine asked. "We didn't mean to crash. It must have been the log's fault." Everyone laughed again.

Seeker, recovering from his laughter, said gently, "We'll take the blame this time, but from now on, you boys will go more slowly until you learn to steer the mover."

"But, Father," insisted Puddly, "Waddler's right. It *is* The Maker's. Maybe we should use it only for Him."

"But how can we do that?" protested Furry-Ball. He could see the end of all his fun.

Tidy-Paw broke into the conversation. "Our Gathering House is a mighty far distance to walk. Maybe The Maker wouldn't mind if Aunt Serenity went there on the mover— especially in cold weather. After all, she's getting up there in years."

They all looked at Aunt Serenity. They hadn't realized how old age had crept up on her, and they were ashamed that they had never even thought of the long walk.

"I'd be glad to pull the mover for you, Aunt Serenity," offered Trasher. They exchanged smiles and nods.

Then, as if Tidy-Paw's remark had unleashed a flood, ideas of how to use the mover for The Maker tumbled out one after another.

"Why not use the mover to collect food for our Gatherings?" suggested Tidy-Paw. "We could get the job done quicker and easier." She said this as Faith and Posie came into the clearing, their paws filled with food.

"And if anyone's sick or injured, we could use it to bring him home," interjected Puddly. "It worked well with Rapid!"

Trasher added his comment. "All those logs for the chairs in our Gathering House—we could haul them much more easily if we used the mover."

Posie and Faith had become part of the conversation by now, and Faith had a suggestion. "We could take food to the hungry by using the mover," she said timidly.

Posie, not to be outdone, added, "And flowers to the sick." But Furry-Ball put an end to the idea sharing. "Won't we ever be able to use the mover just for fun?" he whined.

"Only when it's not being used for The Maker, and only if you're willing to give careful thought to your ways," warned Seeker, pointing to The Book. Furry-Ball and Sunshine nodded in agreement, and soon all of them went quietly back to their tasks.

The subject of the mover had all but been forgotten when Truster spoke up for the first time. "Why don't we tell The Maker about our plans for the mover?" he suggested.

His remark caught them all by surprise, but Waddler was quick to see Truster's point. "That would certainly make us give careful thought to our ways," he assured him.

"We could have a special Gathering and promise The Maker all the things that we'll do with the mover," said Posie excitedly.

"That's exactly what I mean!" exclaimed Truster. "By telling Him all the things that we'll do with the mover, we'll sort of be giving it back to Him." He looked thoughtful for a moment, then added, "And while we're at it, we might as well give Him back anything else that He's given us."

"It's only right," Seeker admitted. "And to begin with, we need to give Him back our Gathering House—He provided it. That's one way to say 'thanks.'"

"And we can also say 'thanks' by giving Him our own selves most of all," acknowledged Trasher. His face expressed the earnestness of his statement, and the rest nodded in agreement.

The issue was settled. A day was decided upon, and preparations were begun. Never had any celebration seemed so special and important. Food was gathered endlessly, decorations were put up in the Gathering House, special translation work was done, and last of all, they took great pains to look their cleanest and neatest. Finally, the day came.

Aunt Serenity rode in style on the flower-decorated mover, while the rest formed a dignified procession behind her. They were just nearing the Gathering House when a familiar face peeked out from behind a tree. It was Rubbish. He had come to see what all the fuss was about. Trying not to be distracted, they filed into the Gathering House. But there he was again, peeking through a window, making them all conscious of the fact that they were being watched.

Waddler opened The Book and translated slowly. "The Upright shall behold his face." He closed The Book reverently and took his seat.

Seeker stood up. "Dear Maker, we are here to give careful thought to our ways, and we want to share these thoughts with You." Beckoning the others to join in a circle around the mover, he continued. "We are here to give You back the mover. We promise to use it for You."

Aunt Serenity rode in style on the flower-decorated mover, while the rest formed a dignified procession behind her.

One by one, they made their promises to The Maker, ending with Sunshine's fervent promise never to speed or crash again.

There was a slight pause, and then Seeker spoke. "Dear Maker, I, Seeker, give myself to You. Methuselah is no longer here to guide this family. I promise to lead them with Your help. I will give thought to my ways." The others, following his example, promised themselves and all that they had to The Maker.

There was another pause, and then Seeker ended their ceremony. "And last of all, Dear Maker, we give You back this Gathering House. It is Yours and to be used only for You. Thank You for providing it."

With that, they all looked up, and though afterward they couldn't say that they had actually seen the face of The Maker, they felt as though they really had, and some even thought that He was smiling.

As for Rubbish, still shaking his head in disbelief, he disappeared from the window and joined the other bandits hiding behind the bushes.

Then, a celebration such as no one had ever seen before took place with decorations and games and storytelling and special food prepared by Aunt Serenity and Tidy-Paw. And when it was over, they all headed for home, taking turns riding on the mover next to Aunt Serenity.

The bandits watched the whole celebration from behind the bushes, and then trudged off toward their hideout on the other side of the brook. They were sullen and in a very bad mood. Complaining to one another, they could not understand why all this "Maker" talk had not stopped when Methuselah died.

CHAPTER 10

The Challenge

"The way of the LORD is strength
for the Upright."
Proverbs 10:29

POSIE SQUINTED. It was a lovely day in May, and she was watching Sarah from her vantage point in the tree overhead. But what was Sarah doing with that long, thin white leaf she was holding? She crept to the end of the branch to get a closer look. It was all so curious. Sarah seemed to be winding it around her tiny Upright—the same one who had come to the tea party long ago. No, on second glance, she was winding it only around her leg—in fact, she had completely covered her leg with the white leaf. It looked so soft and clean. But why was she doing this?

Posie crept out farther. And what she saw puzzled her even more. Sarah was dressed all in white except for a red mark on the white cloth she had on her head. She was bent over the tiny Upright, holding something attached to her ear on one end and the little Upright's chest on the other. Posie was more curious than ever. Then she saw Sarah put a thin sticklike object in the Upright's mouth. She crept out farther. She just had to see what Sarah was doing. Every part of her body strained to see, and then . . .

Crash! The branch snapped and fell, and down with it came Posie. Sarah jumped back in alarm and then, seeing that it was her friend, smiled in relief and leaned forward to welcome her.

Embarrassed about her awkward arrival, Posie stepped out of the tangle of leaves and branches. That is, she tried to step out, but a sharp pain stabbed at her paw and stopped her in her tracks. She winced and tried to walk again, but it hurt so badly that a tear ran down her cheek.

Sarah looked concerned as she moved closer and gently lifted Posie's paw. But Posie winced again, and just as gently, Sarah put

it down. Then she did something strange. She unwound the long white leaf from her tiny Upright and began slowly and ever so gently to wind it around Posie's paw.

At first Posie felt pain and almost withdrew her paw in alarm. But very gradually, the pain disappeared, and soon she felt relief. She wiped her tears and then watched as Sarah tied a knot to hold the white leaf in place. Sarah motioned for her to walk, and so, very cautiously, Posie put her full weight on her hurt paw. Nothing happened. The pain was gone. Oh, her paw felt quite stiff all wound up, but that terrible pain was gone. Sarah had cured her! And now as she watched, her friend was writing what looked like a letter. After attaching it to the white leaf, Sarah waved her customary good-bye, and then watched as Posie waved back and made her way home.

She was a very strange sight as she hobbled stiffly into the clearing with her bound-up paw. So strange that the raccoon family quickly gathered around and bombarded her with questions.

"I don't know why she put this white leaf on," admitted Posie. "But it sure feels a lot better. I think it cured me. And to think that she took it off the tiny Upright and put it on me! Mine must have been a much worse hurt," she said a little proudly.

"Look," said Sunshine, "there's another white leaf. It looks like a letter."

Seeing it, the family detached the letter and set about the task of translating it. Within minutes Waddler had the answer. "It says, 'Come tomorrow,'" he announced.

"Maybe she'll unwind the white leaf if your paw is better," Furry-Ball said hopefully.

Early the next morning they all accompanied Posie to Sarah's meeting spot to await her arrival. At last Sarah came and immediately bent down to inspect the hurt paw. Furry-Ball exchanged knowing glances with the others as Sarah carefully unwound the white leaf. But to everyone's disappointment, Posie winced with pain as she placed her full weight on her paw. Her foot was not cured. Sarah seemed disappointed too. Sighing, she bound it up again and wrote the same message for them all to read. They recognized the words and nodded in understanding. Then all waved good-bye.

For three more days this scene was repeated, until finally the day came when Posie's paw no longer hurt when she took a step.

And when she did, the others let out a cheer. That, in turn, frightened Sarah, and she stepped back in alarm. Then everyone, including Sarah, laughed. They had a lot more to learn about understanding one another, they realized.

How good it felt for Posie to walk normally again! It was as if this were the first time she had ever walked. In fact, she could not stop walking. The family watched in such admiration that they failed to see Sarah winding up the white leaf. Only when she held out her hand to Posie did they notice what was in it— the rolled-up white leaf. She was giving it to her. Posie reached out hesitatingly. Was it really for her? Sarah nodded, and Posie took the gift. And as she felt the softness of the leaf, she sensed its true value. It had cured her, and now it could cure others.

It was Posie who led them all to the Gathering House, and there they told The Maker that the wound-up white leaf was His gift to be used for His service. Then, returning to their home, they stored it next to their most valuable possession—The Book.

Rain fell for the next two days, but they hardly noticed it. Instead, they were totally absorbed in translating and did not think much about the weather. After all, it rained often in the forest, and they were far more interested in what they were translating.

"The way of the Lord is strength for the Upright," read Seeker.

"And *we're* Upright in heart," declared Trasher. "That is, since we follow The Maker," he added.

"And that means that we get stronger when we follow His ways," explained Waddler.

"I wonder what His ways are, though," asked Truster looking out at the rain.

Day after day, more rain fell until they woke up one morning to the sound of rushing water. It was a terrifying sound—one they had never heard before. They looked out. Not far from the base of their tree swirled angry currents of water. The brook had overflowed its banks. And as it did so, it swept up everything it could reach—broken logs and torn off branches—along its path.

It had even pried away loose rocks and devoured them along with other pieces of debris. It was a frightening scene, and they were just about to turn away when an even worse sight caught their eyes. There was Rubbish, desperately clinging to a log being swept along in the current.

"We've got to save him!" shouted Seeker in alarm. In one quick motion, he bounded out the door. Waddler, Trasher, Truster, and Puddly ran after him, and the two youngest raccoons would have joined them had it not been for Posie and Faith who physically held them back.

The others sat there in shock, and the longer they sat, the more fear they felt. They tried not to look out, but it was hard not to hear the angry sounds of the water below. Once they thought they heard a familiar voice calling out, but then it was gone, and they heard it no more.

It was impossible to tell how long they waited, but when their nerves were most frayed, Tidy-Paw reached for The Book. Turning to their latest work, she read, "The way of the Lord is strength for the Upright."

"Surely the way of the Lord is to save Rubbish," reasoned Aunt Serenity. "The Maker will provide them with strength."

Her words brought great comfort to them all until Furry-Ball asked, "But what if Rubbish is hurt? How will they get him home, and how will we help him?"

Rubbish

At that very moment, from down below came the sound of excited voices, and within seconds, Trasher and Puddly came piling in, wet and bedraggled.

"We saved him, but he's too weak to walk, so we came back for the mover," Puddly explained, his teeth chattering from the cold.

"Rubbish gave us some bad news," added Trasher. "He told us that the bandits' hideout was totally destroyed—the flood took the whole tree away. He doesn't know if any of the others made it to safety or not. We thought we heard someone calling on the way back, but we couldn't find him. Try to listen for the voice. We may be able to help when we get back. But right now it will take the two of us to get the mover to Rubbish. The ground is nothing but mud and it's very slippery, but if we turn the mover over, we'll make it." With that, they left.

The rest of the family sat in silence for a long time, listening to the ominous sounds of the water below, while at the same time straining for the sound of a voice. And just when they were beginning to feel that it had only been their imaginations, they heard it distinctly and clearly. "Heeeellllp!" It was a heart-rending cry.

Posie wasted no time in responding. "We have to help whoever it is!" she urged. "It's probably one of the bandits."

"But it isn't safe, Dear," warned Tidy-Paw. "We had better wait until the menfolk get back."

"But it might be too late!" Posie's voice cracked with emotion.

"I'll go with her," said Faith, her mouth quivering as she spoke.

Then they all heard the voice call out again, and it propelled them into action.

"Go quickly," Tidy-Paw urged, and the girls were gone, grabbing the long white leaf as they went.

It seemed to Posie that they would never find him. His voice got weaker and weaker. Trees were falling all around them, creating so much noise that it was difficult for them to even hear each other. When at last they had all but given up hope of finding him, they saw his tail sticking out from under a fallen tree. It was Stealer, and he was seriously hurt.

Posie squeezed under the tree and waited for her eyes to adjust to the darkness. "It's his leg, Faith. It's hurt badly. But there's room enough to wind the white leaf." She reached out for the leaf, and Faith put it into her paw. Expertly, just as she had seen Sarah do, Posie wound it around Stealer's leg. He groaned at first, and then, just as it had for her, the long white leaf began to

Stealer

do its work, and Stealer grew quiet. Posie leaned in Faith's direction, "Go tell the others to come," she urged.

"But I'm afraid to go alone," protested Faith.

"The way of the Lord is strength for the Upright," encouraged Posie. Her voice was filled with assurance.

With that, Faith was gone. And when she returned much later, it was with the others and the mover. Together, they lifted the tree enough to pry Stealer loose and gently laid him on the mover. Then they pulled him to the Gathering House where the others were already giving aid to Rubbish.

The next few days were a blur to them all. Knowing that this was the "way of the Lord," they opened the Gathering House to the hurt and homeless. Aunt Serenity and Tidy-Paw prepared

nourishing food for their patients and guests while Posie and Faith tended to their wounds. Furry-Ball and Sunshine gathered as many dry leaves as they could find for bedding, and the others went out to search for those who were stranded or hurt.

By the time the rain stopped, almost all of the bandits had at one time or another been cared for at the Gathering House. Not one had been lost, thanks to their tireless efforts and The Maker's strength. And of course, Methuselah's example so long ago.

CHAPTER 11

A
New Plan

*Even in a Land of Uprightness they go
on doing evil.*
Isaiah 26:10

B RIGHT SUNSHINE so filled the forest in the next few days that it was hard to believe there had ever been a flood. But in the comings and goings of everyday life, it was impossible to deny the evidence for very long. Trees were uprooted and lay stretched out on the forest floor, and whole logs had been picked up and hurled here and there, landing in strange locations. Mud was everywhere. It was hard to recognize familiar landmarks. Oh, the flood waters had gone down, but the damage would be felt for many days to come.

And yet, they knew that the laws of The Maker were Upright, and so they accepted their circumstances willingly and even a bit cheerfully. And as they went about the task of cleaning up their neighborhood and restoring the Gathering House to its rightful condition, they felt an added sense of accomplishment in having helped their enemies.

"Who knows?" Trasher thought aloud one day. "Maybe they'll see us as friends and come to follow The Maker like Rapid did."

But it just didn't happen that way. Day after day went by. In fact, summer was almost over, and not one of their enemies had come to the Gathering House. But because they found themselves preoccupied with their own projects, they hardly seemed to notice. At last, after many hours of hard work, their land was returned to normal, and hardly a trace of the flood remained. But that was not so in the rest of the forest.

"You should see how things are in enemy territory!" exclaimed Trasher one day after he had been out on a surveying mission with Puddly. "It doesn't look as if they've done one minute of work."

"And they don't even seem to care," complained Puddly. "I suppose they're waiting for us to come and do it for them!" He laughed.

"That's a good idea!" exclaimed Waddler, his face beaming with hope. "Why don't we help them?" He paused for a moment to let it sink in. "We're finished with our work here because we all worked together. They've probably been too busy fighting among themselves."

"You're right, Wad," admitted Trasher. "We did find a group of them, and they were arguing about who would do what. And besides," he added, "some of them are still recovering from the flood. Food is scarce over there in enemy territory—all of them look thin."

"We could use the Upright-mover!" suggested Furry-Ball with pride.

"And we could bring the long white leaf," added Faith. "We still have a little left, and it might help to heal their injuries."

"Perhaps Sarah would give us more," reflected Posie, "if we asked her."

"They'll be a-needin' plenty of healthy food," Aunt Serenity reminded. "And you two can do the gatherin'." She looked at Furry-Ball and Sunshine.

"And before we know it, those bandits may be living in the Land of Uprightness!" Truster said with a big grin. The others chuckled, too, at that thought.

"Not so fast, not so fast," interjected Seeker. He drew down The Book. "We need to go to The Maker for advice." Carefully tracing his paw across the page, his expression changed to one of concern. Then he looked up and began to speak. "It says here that 'even in a Land of Uprightness they go on doing evil.'"

"But why?" questioned Truster, a note of despair in his voice. "We've helped them before, and if we help them again, surely they'll want to follow The Maker like we do."

"It's not that easy, Truster." Seeker's tone was gentle. "But I don't think that should stop us. I think The Maker is telling us not to expect the best from them. After all, they don't follow Him yet. But that shouldn't keep us from doing our part. Let's work out a plan and stick to it no matter what."

He gathered them around him, and together they planned. Then, bowing their heads, they asked The Maker for His strength. They would need it if their enemies continued doing evil, despite their best efforts to make the land Upright.

While Seeker and his helpers headed out with the Upright-mover to start cleaning up, Tidy-Paw and Aunt Serenity instructed Furry-Ball and Sunshine as to what food to gather and where to find it.

Posie and Faith began immediately to write a note to Sarah. They planned to leave it on the wall, but when they arrived, they were surprised to find her already there, playing with her little Uprights. Cautiously coming out of the forest, they handed her their note along with a small piece of the long white leaf—the last they had.

"More, please!" she read aloud in that strange Upright language they had heard before. She was wearing the same white cloth on her head with the strange red mark and a matching white cloth around her waist. Reaching into what looked like her pocket, she drew out another white leaf and a sticklike object and began writing a note to them.

They were disappointed that the note was her only response, but took it and started back on the path to their home. Posie could never bear to wait for very long, and soon she unfolded it and began to translate. "Come back tomorrow," she read. Then she sighed hopefully. "Maybe she *will* give us some more!"

The others had returned by then, and one by one, they reported on the day's events.

"They threw rocks at us and told us to mind our own business!" Truster lamented. "Even Rubbish and Stealer! You'd think at least *they'd* act differently."

"Remember, Son, The Maker warned us that it would be this way." Seeker encouraged them. "Let's keep trying."

"We didn't find very much food," Sunshine admitted. "The flood washed a lot of it away."

"With The Maker's help, you'll find more tomorrow," said Aunt Serenity, trying to comfort them.

"And we didn't get more of the long white leaf," added Posie, "but she said to come back tomorrow."

It was Tidy-Paw who put in a word of encouragement this time. "I wouldn't be at all surprised if she gives you more," she said with a smile.

They went to bed tired that night—a little discouraged and yet with hope that tomorrow would be better. But barely had they fallen asleep than the sound of an intruder woke them all with a start.

"Who's there?" Seeker's protective voice boomed.

"It's me," a faltering voice responded. "Rubbish," the voice continued. "I've come to say I'm sorry." The moon shone on his troubled face. "I couldn't let you think I'd forgotten what you did for me. It's just that . . ." His voice broke off at this point, and then continuing, he said, "I've been one of them for so long . . . and it's awfully hard to stop being one of them. . . . I mean . . . it's not that I want to follow The Maker, you understand. It's just that . . . I had to come and tell you I was sorry. And if you'll come back tomorrow, I'll join you. We need help badly. They won't hurt you as long as I'm with you." He turned to go.

"That's mighty kind of you, Son," Seeker said gently. "We'll take you up on your offer. We'll be there to help you."

They could hardly wait for morning to come. Anxious to get on with their duties, they were up before sunrise. And true to his promise, Rubbish was waiting for them at the edge of enemy territory. Together, using the Upright-mover, they cleared broken tree branches and moved debris into one big pile, working until their bodies ached with exhaustion. From time to time, some of the bandits stepped out to yell insults or make fun of them, but during the course of the day, though they knew that they were being watched, not one other bandit offered to help.

Meanwhile, Posie and Faith returned to the wall surrounding the Big House. Sarah wasn't there, but she had left a package—

"They're just like Sarah's!" exclaimed Posie.

a hard square leaf container filled with more soft white leaves and some other things. They took the items out to examine them, and holding them up, Posie and Faith gasped. They couldn't be—but they were! They were soft and white except for a red mark on two of the items. And though they didn't know the names of these things, they knew exactly what to do with them.

"They're just like Sarah's!" exclaimed Posie.

They put them on their heads and tied them around their waists and then stood for a long time admiring each other and feeling very important. Then they ran home as fast as they could, proudly showing the others their treasures. And though they were tired, they wrote a thank-you note to Sarah.

Later that afternoon, Seeker and his crew returned. "No rocks today," boasted Trasher. "Rubbish was right. They didn't hurt us, but not one came to help."

Undaunted, the next morning back they went. And they continued to go back day after day until gradually enemy terri-

tory was restored to its natural beauty and use. Even the unsightly pile of debris became useful once it was turned into a hospital clinic. Posie and Faith distributed clean white leaves to the injured—among them Stealer, who had not yet recovered from injuries he had gotten during the flood. It wasn't long, however, before he, too, began to look and feel better.

One day, after his recovery, Stealer surprised them as he stepped out of the forest. "I'm here to help," he announced.

And though the rest of the bandits continued doing evil, at least two of their number were trying to live Uprightly.

CHAPTER 12

$\mathcal{S}$aving Life

For whoever desires to save his life will lose it,
but whoever loses his life for My sake
will find it.
Matthew 16:25

F ALL HAD come to the forest, and with it came the cool, crisp days so characteristic of that season. "I'm *so* tired," Posie sighed. Wearing the clean white aprons and caps that Sarah had given them, she and Faith had been working for many days in their clinic, tirelessly arranging their supplies and sweeping the floor to a spotless condition. From time to time, patients came in for treatment, and little by little, injuries were healed, and the sick became well.

Sitting down on a bed to rest, Faith fingered her cap absent-mindedly. Then, taking it off, she laid it on her lap and looked at it with a new interest. "What do you suppose this mark means, and why is it red?" she mused aloud.

Posie bent forward to have a closer look. Then she took off her own cap to compare. Satisfied that they were the same, she thought for a moment and then answered. "I'm not sure, Faith, but the shape looks awfully like The Maker's wooden cross."

"But why is it red?" Faith asked again. "It reminds me of blood, and blood reminds me of sickness and death. I wish it were a different color."

They were both quiet for a while, then Posie looked up. She had an idea. "I think it stands for The Maker's blood, because if The Maker had not died, the Uprights wouldn't have been saved.

Yes, I think Sarah meant this picture to be The Maker's cross stained with His blood. After all, she does follow The Maker."

"But why would she want to remember such an awful thing like The Maker's death?" Faith shook her head in disbelief.

"But don't you understand?" Posie leaned forward and touched the red cross on Faith's cap. "The Maker's death isn't awful—it's wonderful! He loved them so much that He gave His life for them, and without His death, they'd still have masks on their hearts. They could never be Upright by themselves. It took His death to save them. And I think Sarah always wants to remember that." Posie thought for a moment. "And besides, because The Maker gave His life for theirs, He must be *against* sickness and death. He wants Uprights to live, not die, and when Sarah helps to heal, she's serving The Maker."

Faith took all this in. For a moment she was quiet. At last she nodded. "I think you're right, Posie. And I think she wants us to help heal sickness and save lives too. That must be why she gave us these things to wear. It *is* good to think about The Maker's death, even though it makes me feel sad."

It would be hard to say how long they sat there thinking about all of these things, but suddenly, they were conscious of a dark shadow blocking the doorway. They looked up to see the familiar face of Stealer. His head hung low, and he did not speak.

Posie addressed him. "Are you sick, Stealer? Does your injury hurt again?" He did not answer. He seemed embarrassed or ashamed—they couldn't tell which.

"Don't be afraid to tell us what's wrong," encouraged Faith.

"It's . . . it's not me," he answered.

"Well, then, who is it?" Posie questioned him eagerly.

"I don't know. . . . That is, I *do* know. . . . I mean, I don't know her name." He hung his head even lower.

Posie and Faith exchanged glances. They were very perplexed. "Please tell us what's wrong!" they blurted out.

Stealer stepped back. He turned and would have fled in fear, but Posie reached out and grabbed his tail.

"Stealer, please! We don't mean to frighten you. We just want to help. And someone you know needs help. Please tell us who it is."

He turned back and came toward them slowly. "You're right," he admitted. "It's just that . . . after all you did for me, I just couldn't pass her up. She'll die without help. She's too tiny to make it."

"Who, Stealer? Who?" begged Faith, her voice shaking with emotion.

"She's just a runt," he answered. "They leave them to die all the time in our country. Not enough food for all of them, so they leave the littlest one to die. But maybe if you help her, she'll make it." His face looked hopeful. "That is, if it's not too late."

"We'll follow you," announced Posie, putting on her cap.

"But wait!" Faith answered weakly. "If we go farther into enemy territory, it would be dangerous. We might even die."

Posie looked at her imploringly. "But if we don't go, *she* might die! Faith, don't you remember? We serve The Maker now. He gave His life for His enemies. Shouldn't we risk ours? The Maker will take care of us! If you won't go, I'll go alone."

Faith hung her head. Fear had overtaken her, and she could not move. Posie looked at her sadly, then turned to follow Stealer. Soon they were out of sight.

True to his name, Stealer crept softly and noiselessly through the forest. Posie lost track of time and even the direction in which they were going, so intent was she on following him. But when a twig snapped behind her, she stopped, frozen in her tracks. At this point she would have gladly turned back had she remembered the way, but instead, she stood there and weakly called out, "Stealer!" Though almost out of sight, Stealer heard her voice and returned to her side.

"I heard something," she whispered. They listened together intently until at last they heard another sound—the sound of soft padded footsteps. They stood motionless and, preparing for the worst, looked toward the sound. Out of the darkness stepped a small figure.

"I couldn't let you go alone," a trembling voice spoke up. It was Faith.

Relieved, the two raccoons hugged and comforted each other, and were soon off again following Stealer. The forest grew darker and darker. Nothing was recognizable to them. They were totally dependent on Stealer's memory, but somehow they felt the worst was over, and continued on with a new determination.

At last, from up ahead came Stealer's voice. "Hurry! Here she is!"

Joy

They ran forward with one last burst of energy. And when they found him, Stealer was bending over something very tiny—so tiny that at first they could not make out any features. Then it moved. They heard a pitiful little whimper, and then all was quiet again. Posie reached out to touch the little body, and as she did so, she felt the tiniest heartbeat imaginable.

"Quick, Stealer, get some water," she urged. He turned and in a second was gone.

Faith leaned over and touched the baby's fur very gently. "Did you ever see anything so tiny?" she asked in amazement. To their surprise, the baby moved, as if responding to Faith's touch.

This time Posie stroked her fur. "Can you imagine anyone wanting to leave this tiny little one? Don't they know that all life is precious—even little lives? Whoever left her has no heart."

Faith nodded in agreement. "I think she's cold," she said, noticing her movements. "She only moves when our warm paws touch her. Let's cover her with our warm fur," she suggested. Together, they did. And by the time Stealer arrived with water, he found them holding a whimpering, wiggling mass of fur.

Only with all three of them working together were they successful in getting several drops of water down her little throat. But soon it was clear that the tiny baby would make it with their help, and they quickly made plans to take her back to the clinic.

The rest they couldn't remember—the long, hard trip back, the endless stopping on the way to gently trickle water into the baby's mouth—none of it really mattered to them. What did matter was that their lives were not nearly as important as saving this little one's life. And when at last they tucked her into a cozy bed, they knew a little of what The Maker had suffered when He gave His life for the lost Uprights, and a little of what Methuselah had felt when he decided to give his life to save Rabid's.

The life that someone else had considered worthless, they saw as precious, and they were happy to have had a part in saving that little life.

CHAPTER 13

The
*U*nwilling Missionary

He whose walk is Upright fears the LORD.
Proverbs 14:2

P UDDLY WAS sulking again! Weren't they doing enough already? As he walked along, he kicked a rock and muttered to himself some more. After all, they had started a Gathering House and a clinic, and they were even carrying on relief work after the flood. Why did Waddler insist on going even further—"to share The Maker with those in foreign countries," as he put it? Who would "share The Maker" with their enemies right here if he were to go with Waddler? And besides, it was dangerous going off into unknown countries. You could get killed by foreigners or, worse yet, by foreign Uprights. And the cold. Winter was almost upon them. It was far too cold to be traveling to unknown countries. And what about food? Who could say what you would end up having to eat!

He kicked another rock. Just thinking about Waddler's final argument angered him all the more. Why did Waddler have to bring The Book into it? Sure, he saw the words himself: "Let all the Upright in heart praise him!" But did that mean that you should rush off and share The Maker with those in foreign countries, especially when you weren't finished doing it at home?

No, he would serve The Maker right here, thank you! It wasn't that he couldn't be a team player—it was that he totally disagreed with Waddler and the rest. They'd find out that he was right. And when they all died from starvation or were killed by those foreigners, only he and Seeker would be left to take care of the family. Puddly sighed. Then they'd see that he was the true hero.

Having convinced himself that he had made the right choice, he looked up. The stone wall lay before him and beyond that, the Big House. He crept toward it with a new hope in his heart. Maybe he could learn something new by watching the Uprights inside. And if Waddler, Trasher, and Truster decided to be foreign missionaries, and if they ever returned alive, they would see that the work here had moved forward because of the new ideas that he had gathered. Yes, someone had to carry on the work at home, and he was that someone.

He climbed a small fir tree alongside one of the clear stone openings. Straining every muscle, he found that by leaning out he could just peek through the lowest opening. He caught his breath. There in the front of the room was an evergreen tree. A tree *inside?* He had never noticed one inside before. And this was not just any plain, old tree. This one was covered with the most beautiful decorations he had ever seen. He hung there for a moment trying to take it all in. The trees in the forest could not compare with this one. Never had he seen such sparkling things on a tree. But the top attracted him the most. Shining as if it had been plucked right out of the sky itself, a golden star was perched right on the very top of the tree.

"How do these Uprights do such amazing things?" he wondered aloud. But before he could think any further, beautiful sounds floated out through the clear stone opening. He listened, carefully trying to remember each note to share with the others. He even tried to copy the sound, but only squeaks and grunts came out. "Well, at least I can tell them what a star looks like up close, and how it shines and lights up the whole Big House. And to think—they put it on a tree. They must love the forest too."

Filled with all this news, Puddly scampered down and headed for home. Yes, more and more, he knew that he had made the right choice. Waddler, Trasher, and Truster could "go forward" and claim new ground for The Maker, but he, Puddly, knew that there was plenty to do right here, and he planned to do it, even if he had to do it all by himself.

He walked briskly with a spring in his steps, recapturing the image of that beautiful star in his mind. "I wonder why they put it on *top* of the tree," he reflected. Then, answering his own question, he spoke aloud. "Well, to see it better, and so that it will give out more light. After all, it wouldn't shine nearly as much if it were under a branch," he concluded.

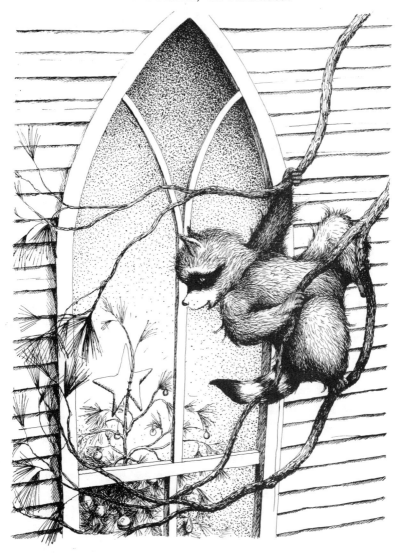

His thoughts were suddenly interrupted by Upright voices. Scooting under a young fir tree, he crouched absolutely still, straining to see and hear what he could. To get a better view, he climbed up the trunk and out onto a branch. Very carefully, he poked his head through the boughs. There, just a short distance away, were two very large Uprights. And then came the worst shock of all—a terrifying clanging and screeching sound that sent chills down his spine. He closed his eyes and covered his ears with his paws, but it was no use. Still that piercing sound reached him, and then a sickening crack of a nearby tree, followed by an even more sickening THUD! He opened his eyes and saw what he had instinctively dreaded—a beautiful fir tree lying on the ground close by—cut down by those Uprights with their terrible tree-killer.

He stifled a sob. "What right do they have to do that?" he protested. As he watched, the Uprights flung it on a pile of freshly cut trees. Then they came closer and started on another tree. "Pretty soon there won't even be a forest!" Puddly wailed. "Don't they know that it takes time to grow a forest?" He shuddered as the tree hit the ground. "That was one of my favorite climbing trees too!" he muttered. He began to feel uneasy. Those Uprights were getting too close for comfort. He was just looking around for an escape route, in case they came his way, when they *did.*

What followed next happened so quickly that Puddly never had a chance to escape. He simply sat there, frozen to the branch in fear, and when the tree came down, he came with it. Regaining his senses after the crash of the tree, he struggled to free himself from the tangle of branches. He wasn't hurt, but he was terribly frightened. Perhaps this panic kept him from escaping. But try as he would, he could not find his way out. And the next thing he knew, the entire pile of trees was being lifted up and dumped onto a flat thing, and he was a part of that pile.

At last he again managed to poke through the branches and was within seconds of escape when another noise caused him to freeze. This time it wasn't a screeching noise, but it was loud and accompanied by a terrible jolt. And then his worst fears were realized—he was on some sort of an Upright-mover. The whole pile of trees, with him in it, was moving—at first slowly, then little by little, faster than he had ever moved in his life. And as the Upright-mover picked up speed, he realized that he was going far away, and he might never see his home again.

Puddly was terrified. If only the Upright-mover would slow down, then he could jump off and find his way back. But the

mover only went faster, dashing all hope that he would ever see his family again. Numbness set in—the kind of numbness that comes from sudden shock. Puddly had never felt so alone before. But then he remembered. He was not alone. The Maker was with him. He had helped him before. Maybe He would help him now.

He said the words aloud: "Help me, Dear Maker." And then, just as he said those words, a thought entered his mind: *Why not*

carefully watch the way the mover went—just in case The Maker did help? All at once, the fear left, and in its place came a calmness— in fact, such a calmness that Puddly suddenly felt quite brave. Though the mover took him farther and farther away, he watched every turn, and he knew he could find his way back.

It seemed like hours went by, but the mover never slowed down. Puddly was tired and hungry, but still he kept his vigil— watching the way the mover went, waiting for his opportunity to escape. He knew that to jump off would mean sure death. But he didn't know how much longer he could keep his eyes open.

He was at the point of total exhaustion and just starting to close his eyes when the mover came to an abrupt halt. Puddly burrowed deep into the pile of branches to hide. And as the Uprights unloaded the trees from the mover, they never suspected that a passenger was hiding among them. At last they completed their task and left.

Puddly could almost taste freedom, but he was too tired to start his long trip back. He felt much safer now that the Uprights were gone, and so instead, he climbed deeper under the pile, curled up into a ball, and fell fast asleep.

He was still sleeping the next day when some more Uprights came. They selected the very tree in which Puddly slept and placed his tree on another mover, rudely awakening him in the process. Despair now filled his heart. If only he had not fallen asleep. He had been so close to freedom!

But again, refusing to give in to this feeling, he called upon The Maker and carefully watched the way the mover went. This time, the trip was short, and Puddly, wide awake by now, clung to his tree as it was dumped out of the mover onto the cold ground. He looked around him. There were Uprights walking around on flat square rocks, movers making loud noises, lots of Big Houses (not at all like the Big House back home), but not one single tree. Suddenly, he knew beyond any doubt that he was in a *very* foreign country. It even smelled strange. In fact, it smelled almost nasty.

He had just buried himself under a bough, so as not to be seen, when he felt the tree being lifted to a standing position. Upright voices sounded like they were very close, and all of a sudden he was aware of some movement that began at the top of the tree. The Uprights were putting something onto the branches. And then he saw it—a long green rope, being wound around the tree by Upright hands. He edged his way upward and found a hiding place, and there he stayed for what seemed forever until at last darkness came.

Then, just as his moment of escape had arrived, a loud chorus of Upright voices interrupted him. Somehow that noise sounded familiar to him. Where had he heard that before? He edged his way out on a branch, but still finding it impossible to see clearly, he climbed higher—so high that he found himself next to a golden object shaped exactly like the star he had seen on the tree in the Big House.

Suddenly, it hit him. The star *was* the same as he had seen in the Big House, and so was the noise. It was exactly the same! Could it be that these Uprights in this foreign country followed The Maker too? Maybe they didn't have a Big House, and this was the best they could do.

He was putting together the pieces of this puzzle when a very bright light blinded him. It was so bright that at first he could not see the source. Then, to his absolute horror, he saw that it came from the star next to him, making him clearly visible to all the Uprights.

It would be impossible to describe Puddly's shock as the star was illuminated, except to say that the shock was greater still on the faces of the Uprights who watched the lighting of their Christmas tree. Puddly looked down. Other lights had also come on all over the tree. Now there was no place to hide. Oh, how he wished he were invisible! But the truth of the matter was that he was very visible, and yet he clung to his branch as if he were glued there.

It wasn't until a young girl called out to her mother, "Mommy, can we have a Christmas raccoon on top of our tree?"

that Puddly came to his senses. He knew that all eyes were upon him, and he did not like it one bit. Deciding that it was now or never, he dashed down the tree, and before the Uprights knew what was happening, he disappeared through the crowd, leaving the tree raccoonless at last.

CHAPTER 14

ℋaving
a Prayer

The prayer of the Upright is His delight.
Proverbs 15:8

PUDDLY WAS hungry and thirsty and very tired, but nothing could stop him now. Running until he thought his legs would fall off, he didn't rest until he came to some trees and bushes. There he collapsed in a heap, glad to be away from the cold flat rocks of the Uprights.

He lay there for a long time panting, until he heard what sounded like a brook. He moved toward the sound, and finding it, he drank deeply of the cool water. Then, ravenous with hunger, he looked around for food. He remembered how he had felt before about foreign food, but all that he knew now was that he was so hungry he could eat anything, and he did. Grabbing some dried berries and other things that he had never seen before, he ate until he was stuffed and then slept for a long, long time.

When at last he awoke, he felt refreshed and ready for his trip back. But before he started out, he bowed his head once more. "Thank You, Dear Maker. You *did* help, and I know You'll help me get home safely."

The weather was cold and the trip was tiring, and there were times when Puddly lost his way. But a simple prayer to The Maker, and soon he was back on the trail again.

Although on his journey he never again came into contact with Uprights, he thought much about his encounter with them. He remembered how he had felt when the star at the top of the tree was lit up. He hadn't wanted any of the Uprights to see him. But like it or not, there he was with the light shining on him.

Suddenly, he understood. "Just as I was unwilling to be seen shining like a light, I was also unwilling to go to a foreign country and shine for The Maker—like the star on top of the tree." Feeling very ashamed, he vowed right there that he would go wherever The Maker sent him.

A few nights later he began to understand what his promise might mean, when he came upon his first "foreigners." There were two gangs of them, and they were fighting. Shaking with fear, and yet still curious, he climbed a tree to get a good look at them. He was shocked at what he saw.

They were raccoons, all right, except for one thing. There was something distinctly different about them. Was that *brown* that he saw in their tails, or was he just imagining it? He looked at his own tail—gray and white and black—and felt relieved. Now *there* was a normal tail! He looked again from one foreigner to another and discovered to his horror the terrible truth—they *did* have brown in their tails.

Soon, however, he was appalled to discover something even more unsettling. They spoke differently. Now and then he recognized a word or two, but for the most part, he could not understand them.

Puddly sighed. Other than these differences, they seemed just like the bandits at home. *Perhaps they were not so different after all,* he thought. He even began to feel a little sorry for them. *It isn't their fault,* he reminded himself. *They just don't know The Maker— no one's ever told them.* He'd have to tell the others about them when he got back. And then remembering his vow, he went one step further. *I guess I could show the others where these foreign bandits live,* he decided.

The journey was long and hard, but at last he arrived home. It would be difficult to describe the reaction of the family the day Puddly walked into the clearing. Since he'd been gone for so long, the family had feared the worst—that he was dead. They had grieved, knowing nothing of what had happened. Now, it was as if he had returned from the dead, and it took Puddly a long time to convince them that he hadn't.

When they had gotten over their shock and had expressed their joy at seeing him alive again, Puddly told them his story. He told them of the star on the top of the tree in the Big House, and then of how quite by mistake he had become the star on the top of a tree in a foreign country. But last of all, he described to them what the foreign raccoons looked like and how they talked.

"I want to be a willing light," he confessed to them all. "I guess you might say The Maker has made me willing."

"Grandfather would have been very proud to hear you say that, Son," said Seeker, giving him a pat.

The next morning, Puddly was up before any of the others, and by the time Posie came down, he was busily setting the table. She noticed this change from his old pattern right away. He had never set the table before.

"You seem different somehow, Puddly," she commented, picking up some shells and placing them on the table.

"I'm really the same except in one way," he began to explain.

"What's that, Puddly?"

"Well, inside I feel different. I mean . . . I can't forget them—those foreign bandits. It isn't what they look like. They're different, of course, but inside they're really just like us. It's . . ." Puddly brushed a tear from his eye. "It's that . . . without knowing The Maker, they don't have a prayer."

"Now they will," said Posie matter-of-factly.

"What do you mean?" Puddly looked up questioningly.

"I mean that from now on you'll be praying for them," she answered. "You're different now, Puddly, and I believe The Maker will answer your prayer." Posie smiled—a smile of encouragement.

He smiled back and said, "You're right, Posie. I will pray."

Just then noises from above interrupted their conversation, and one by one, the others came down for breakfast. They were a little surprised to see Puddly up so early, but they were glad that he was safely home at last and eagerly listened to him recount his adventures. Even more wonderful to them, however, was that somehow he seemed changed. He looked the same, yet he was

very different. It was as though all that he had seen and heard had been deeply etched in his heart, and he was filled with a sense of mission and purpose that he never had before.

Waddler, Trasher, and Truster listened to Puddly's plan that they go and tell the foreigners about The Maker. They agreed heartily and were glad that he had come to this decision himself, but they seemed especially interested in Puddly's description of the foreigners.

"You say their tails were a different color, Puddly?" Trasher questioned. "Theirs were *brown?*" His voice had a note of disdain. Then his expression softened as if he had just remembered something. "Well, I suppose it's not important. After all, The Maker created them too."

Furry-Ball broke in at this point. "That's right, and if flowers are different colors, why can't tails be different colors? And besides, even if you don't have a tail, you're really not different—inside, that is." He looked over at Waddler.

An uncomfortable silence followed, and the conversation would have ended right there had not Puddly brought up a new angle.

"But we can't overlook their different language." His words got their attention, and all eyes turned to Puddly. He continued, "I don't mean that we shouldn't accept their language. I mean that we'll have to find a way to learn how to speak to them." They sat there silently thinking about this. Never had they spoken any language but their own.

"You're right, Son," agreed Seeker, who had been listening to their conversation. "If The Maker went to all the trouble of becoming an Upright and speaking Upright language, the least we can do is to learn the language of those foreign raccoons. They deserve the chance to know The Maker too."

"But how can we do that, Father?" asked Trasher.

"Well, to start with, by praying for them," he said as he opened The Book. Posie and Puddly exchanged knowing glances. "The prayer of the Upright is His delight," he translated. "And right now's as good a time as any to begin." Seeker motioned for them to join him in a circle.

It seemed the right thing for them to do—to pray for those foreign bandits even though they might be enemies. After all, had not Methuselah died for an enemy? And so they joined paws and hearts and prayed. And as they did so, they were unaware of the fact that never before in the forest had there been anything like this—a raccoon prayer meeting for foreign bandits.

CHAPTER 15

eflections

Praise befits the Upright.
Psalm 33:1

I T HAD started with prayer. But that was only the beginning, because as they prayed each day, they grew to care more and more about the foreign bandits even if they did look and speak so differently. And caring as they did, they simply had to find a way to tell them of The Maker and give them the chance to follow Him. Even foreigners deserved to hear.

Winter was well upon them, and it was not a good time to be thinking of venturing out, but Puddly couldn't stop himself one day after they prayed. "I can't get away from the idea that The Maker wants me to put feet on my prayers. I think He wants me to go there and live with them," he said. "If I could learn to translate the Upright language by using The Code, I know I could learn their language, and then I could translate The Book and . . ."

Waddler interrupted with a laugh. And once he started, he could not stop. Only when Puddly's expression turned to hurt did Waddler stop and explain what was so funny. "A few months ago, Puddly, you told us that you didn't think *we* should go as missionaries to foreign countries, and now it'll be hard to stop *you!* It's still winter, remember!"

Puddly looked embarrassed. It was altogether true. He smiled at the humor of it and then got very quiet.

"But you're right, Puddly," Waddler said, picking up where he had left off. "We could go in teams and live with them and learn their languages. There must be many more foreigners than just the ones you saw. And I say that as soon as the weather gets a bit warmer, we start!"

"Can I go too?" asked Furry-Ball, almost exploding with excitement.

"No, Furry," Waddler answered. His voice took on a gentle tone. "It would be too dangerous for you to go. You see, they might not accept us." Furry-Ball looked disappointed.

Seeker spoke up. "Puddly's idea is a good one, but Waddler is right. It would be dangerous. Only us menfolk should go."

"Father," Trasher added his suggestion, "we can't all go! Someone needs to stay home and protect the family. Wouldn't it be better if only the single men went? I, for one, would be willing to go." His face reflected his determination.

Seeing the logic of his argument, Seeker agreed.

Then Waddler spoke up. "And I wouldn't miss this opportunity for anything!"

"Well, that makes three," said Seeker encouragingly.

"I want to go too," declared Truster.

Seeker smiled broadly. "Looks like we have two teams! And while you're living in foreign countries learning new languages, we'll be carrying on the work here."

Waddler looked over at Furry-Ball. "You look so disappointed, Furry, but remember, there's a really important job at home that only you can do for us while we're gone," he said.

Furry-Ball looked up expectantly. "Did you say *important?*" he asked.

"Yes, Furry." Waddler looked very intently at him and the rest of the family. "We're only willing to go if you all pray for us every day while we're gone. And it'll take all of your prayers to keep us safe and enable us to get our job done. Your job of praying for us is really more important than our job of going to foreign countries."

Furry-Ball beamed. "Do you really think so, Wad?" he asked. Waddler nodded. "Well, then, you can count on me," Furry-Ball promised.

One by one, the rest of the family added their promises, and then Seeker took out The Book. He began translating.

"Praise befits the Upright."

"What does that mean, Father?" questioned Posie.

"It means that it's the right thing for us who are Upright in heart to praise The Maker," he explained. "Let's do that," he encouraged them. "We have a lot to praise Him for this morning."

Together they bowed their heads, and Seeker spoke to The Maker. "Dear Maker, the idea to live with our enemies is from You because we'd never try this on our own. We're asking You to give safety and strength to the boys as they go. We can praise You ahead of time for the work You'll do in the hearts of our enemies." With that, he looked up and smiled. "And now we have lots to do to get our menfolk ready," he announced.

And there was a lot to do. While the family gathered and packed food and supplies, the soon-to-be missionaries planned their strategy and mapped out their route. They would follow the brook as far as they could, and at the point where it joined the larger stream, they would separate. Waddler and Trasher would stay in the country nearby, and Puddly and Truster would continue to go north to the country where Puddly had been. Though it would be difficult to pull the Upright-mover, they decided to take it in order to carry their supplies more easily and to provide transportation in case of injury.

During all of this planning, Posie was quiet. She did not like to think about the long separation this would mean to their family. But what she dreaded most was not being able to communicate. And so it was that Posie thought of a clever idea for the missionaries to communicate with the family while they were gone. Since the brook ran south, she reasoned, the missionaries could depend on the flow of the stream to carry their messages as they traveled. And once a code was devised, they could communicate such messages as, "Things are going well," "We're in danger," "We're running into trouble," "One of us is hurt," or

"The job is done." To do this they would scratch their symbols on tree bark and float them downstream. The family, at their end, would place a tree limb across the brook to catch everything that floated down. They agreed to look daily for messages among all the debris that collected.

Posie and Waddler decided to test out this message system one day. With great anticipation, Posie, stationed by the tree limb, spotted a piece of tree bark floating down toward her. Excitedly, she reached out and grabbed it. Sure enough, a message was carefully scratched upon it. Then two more tree bark messages floated down, confirming the first message. Waddler appeared a few minutes later, and Posie blurted out in excitement, "The message says that the job is done!"

Waddler smiled smugly. "The system works perfectly."

Posie sighed. "Oh, Waddler," she looked at him with a serious expression, "if only the job were already done. It seems so dangerous." Then catching herself, she reminded them both, "Yet as far as The Maker is concerned, the job *is* done. We can praise Him already."

"You're right, Posie. And praise befits us who are Upright in heart. And do you know something else?"

"What?" she asked expectantly.

"Praise especially befits you." He was smiling as he looked at her. Not understanding exactly what he meant, she looked away in embarrassment. He grew quiet, then added, "When I'm gone, it will help me so much to know that you are here praying and receiving our messages and giving praise to The Maker for a job already done."

"Oh, I will," she promised him fervently. "Every day I'll pray."

Several weeks went by. When at last the weather grew warmer, the date was set for the departure of the missionaries. There were tears on both sides as they expressed their farewells. But finally, it was Seeker's prayer for them all that brought comfort, and the two teams left. The rest of the family just stood there for a while trying to get used to the idea that almost half of their members were gone, and then, one by one, they began to go about their daily chores.

Posie and Faith headed for the clinic to check on their small patient. Stealer had been caring for her when they were away. "I think I'll stop by the brook to see if there are any messages yet," suggested Posie on the way.

Faith looked at her in astonishment. "They've only just left! You can look, but I doubt whether they would have sent a message so soon!" she said with a shrug. Then reluctantly, she announced, "I'm going on ahead."

Undaunted, Posie turned toward the brook. "I'll catch up with you later," she called. Then, spurred on by her hope, she ran to the place they had agreed on as the message center. Her heart sank. She scanned every inch of water and even waded out into the quiet pool created by the tree limb they had stretched across, but not one piece of bark was to be seen. She picked up several sticks and threw them out of the way. She was just about to leave when she noticed her reflection in the pool.

A cool breeze blew across the water, blurring her picture and causing her image to be distorted into a strange new creature. She laughed aloud, then bent down to get a better look. The breeze stopped, almost instantly calming the water, and instead of a strange creature, she saw herself as she really was. She studied her reflection. Her glossy fur, now long and thick, shone in the sunlight. Her eyes sparkled, and her delicate paws became a graceful extension of the water. Turning slightly, she took note of her tail, luxurious by now and resplendent with dark, rich rings.

To tell the truth, Posie had never noticed herself before. And now, for the first time, she did, and she enjoyed every detail she

saw. She turned this way and that in an attempt to see herself in a new way—even moving her wreath in several different positions with the hope that she could find the most flattering way to wear it. When she tired of looking at herself in different positions, she simply sat there on the tree limb and stared at herself.

I wonder what Waddler meant when he said that praise especially befit me, she mused. *Does he think I'm beautiful? Could it be my wreath or my tail or . . . maybe it's just my imagination,* she thought.

She was in the process of admiring herself as she turned her head this way and that, when suddenly she heard a noise behind her. Startled, she looked up to find Faith staring at her in disgust.

"I thought you said you would catch up with me." Her voice had an irritated note to it. "I've already been to the clinic, and here you are still at the brook. Was there a message?"

"No . . . no, there was no message," Posie admitted.

"Well, then, what's taken you so long? I already checked on our little baby, and she's doing fine. I think Stealer actually enjoys taking care of her. What have you been doing here?" Faith paused, and then, as if answering her own question, she said in relief, "Oh, you've been praying for them. That's what you've been doing!"

Posie did not want to admit the truth, so she said nothing. She felt more ashamed than she had ever felt in her life, and yet she couldn't bring herself to tell Faith what she had really been doing—admiring her own reflection. And though on the walk back, she expressed interest in all that Faith had done, she felt empty and cheated for having missed out on the visit to their newest patient. But at the same time, she felt strangely drawn to her reflection, and she wondered if Waddler had really noticed her in a special way.

As Posie fell asleep that night, she felt ashamed that she had not kept her promise to Waddler, especially when this had been the very first day. Somehow it all reminded her of her broken promise to Methuselah so long ago. She had told Grandfather she was sorry, and he had told her that he forgave her. If only she could tell Waddler that she was sorry, but that was impossible. Turning to the only One she could, she said, "I'm sorry, Dear Maker." Tomorrow she would keep her promise, she vowed, and at last she slept.

CHAPTER 16

The *H*ighway of the Upright

The highway of the Upright
is to depart from evil.
Proverbs 16:17

A MESSAGE!" Posie shouted aloud, startling a bird nearby. It was early the next morning, and she had come to the brook, determined to keep her promise of the night before. Plunging heedlessly into the water, she reached for the piece of bark. Her eyes devoured every word. "All is well," she read, and sighing in relief, she pressed the wet bark to her heart. She sighed again. Then, remembering her promise, she climbed onto the tree limb and began to pray.

"Dear Maker, I promised Waddler that I would pray every day, and here I am." She had barely gotten the words out of her mouth when her thoughts were interrupted. *If there's one message, couldn't there be another?* she wondered and decided to check just in case. She looked down into the pool of water. There was no message—only a few leaves and twigs. She was just about to return to praying when she caught a glimpse of something else— her reflection.

Perhaps it was because she wasn't expecting to see her reflection at that moment and got distracted from her promise, or maybe it was because seeing herself right then became more important to her than keeping her promise, but she totally forgot her vow. Instead she gazed intently at herself. *Maybe it is true,* she thought. *Maybe Waddler does think I'm beautiful.* And the more she looked, the more she felt sure that he did.

She was so absorbed in her reflection that the piece of bark fell right out of her hand and made a splash as it hit the water. She picked it up and read it again carefully. "It's definitely Puddly's handwriting," she said wistfully. "Maybe Waddler will write tomorrow," she whispered to herself.

Posie gasped. She was shocked at her own words. It was as if someone else had said them. And yet she had heard herself very clearly. Why did she wish that Waddler would write? She looked down at her reflection, and as if talking to another person, she demanded an answer. "Well?" she asked indignantly. No answer came, but gradually, her expression softened and then changed to utter dismay. She felt so confused and ashamed of her

feelings. *It's not that I don't care about the others,* she tried to convince herself. She sighed, but it was no use pretending. So, looking herself right in the eye, she admitted, *But I do so care about Waddler—in a different way.* There—the truth was out, and though she felt better, it was still very confusing to her and a little exciting and frightening all at the same time.

Then, still looking at her reflection, a new thought occurred to her. *Does it show?* she wondered, and she searched her reflection carefully for any clues. *No. No one could possibly know,* she assured herself. *And I'll keep it a secret,* she decided.

The thought of Waddler made her stare at her reflection for a long time. How she hoped that he thought she was beautiful! Again and again, she went over his words, trying to discover any hidden meaning that she could. "Praise especially befits you," he had said. But in the end, she had to admit that he probably did not see her any differently from his own sister, Faith.

No sooner had she thought of Faith than another thought crossed her mind. "Oh, no!" she said, "I forgot all about Faith! We were supposed to go to the clinic!" Looking quickly at the sun, she tried to estimate how long she had been there, and hurrying as fast as she could, she raced home with the piece of bark. The family was glad to get the message that all was well. But Seeker's remark made her uncomfortable.

"A real answer to your prayers, Posie, but sorry you missed our morning translation."

Then Tidy-Paw's comment made her even more uncomfortable. "Faith thought you might be praying, and so she left without you."

Posie looked down in embarrassment. How could she admit that all she had done was to admire her reflection and wish that Waddler had sent her a message? She could not bear to tell them that she had not prayed at all, and so instead, she apologized for missing the translation of The Book, and excused herself to catch up with Faith.

But by the time she got to the fork in the path, she had gotten over the embarrassment and felt relieved that she had kept her secret. She had no idea that she was becoming hardened, and so when her feet headed straight for the tree limb in the brook, she justified herself with the thought, *Just one quick look, in case there's another message.*

Her eyes scanned the pool for a piece of bark, and finding none, without so much as a thought, she bent over to see her

reflection. Her fur, she noticed, was slightly ruffled from protruding branches, so she spent some time smoothing it into place. *Much better,* she had to admit. Then she checked her long white whiskers. A cobweb hung untidily from them, and so she combed it out with her paws. In doing so, she found some clumps of dirt stuck between her toes. Somehow, dirt clumps seemed out of place on her otherwise clean appearance, so she brushed them off.

She was so busy with her efforts that she failed to notice a small piece of bark drifting downstream, and had it not bumped right into her foot dangling from the tree limb, she might have missed it altogether. Startled by it at first, she looked down and, in one quick motion, grabbed it from the water. "Thank you for praying. Waddler," she read aloud.

Instead of being happy to get this message from Waddler, Posie reacted quite strangely. She sat down on the tree limb and sobbed. She sobbed for such a long time that her eyes were red and her fur was wet with tears. And when at last her sobbing was over, she wiped her eyes and looked down at the water. A breeze had come up, and the pool, once quiet, was rippled, distorting her reflection.

"You!" she accused herself angrily. "It's your fault. You haven't prayed for Waddler at all!" Another sob escaped, and pointing at herself, she added more insults. "This is what you

really look like!" she cried as she viewed her distorted image. "You're not beautiful at all—you're ugly!" She cried some more. Then, feeling more miserable than she had since Methuselah died, she rocked back and forth with her paws covering her eyes, moaning and sobbing as if her heart would break.

That was how Faith found her when she stopped at the brook on her way home. Fearing the worst, she blurted out, "What's wrong, Posie? Has something happened to them?" Posie handed her the message numbly. Reading it, Faith felt more confused than ever. "What's wrong? He's just thanking you for your prayers. I don't understand."

"That's just it," moaned Posie. "I haven't prayed." She sobbed some more.

"Haven't prayed?" Faith stared incredulously. "I thought that's why you came here." Her words trailed off in unbelief.

"I came here to look at my reflection." The truth was out. Posie hung her head in shame.

Faith looked at her with a hurt expression. "But why?" she pressed. "We have so much to do, and The Maker's counting on us to do it, and you came here to look at your reflection?" She shook her head in disbelief. "I just don't understand."

Posie looked over at Faith. Her fur was disheveled, cobwebs hung from one ear, and clumps of dirt covered her feet. But to Posie at that moment, Faith looked beautiful. Here was a friend who had spent the morning caring for their patients all by herself, and now here was this friend trying to understand her and her selfish actions. All of a sudden, in seeing Faith's beauty, Posie saw herself in contrast, and she felt more ugly than ever. "You'll hate me, Faith," she warned.

With a tender expression, Faith reached over and took her hand. "No, I won't. I promise. Tell me what's wrong, Posie."

"Well, at first I didn't come here to see my reflection," she assured her. "It was only after I began to think of something Waddler said that I began to notice myself."

Faith sighed. "I think I'm beginning to understand."

Posie continued, and before she knew it, her whole secret had slipped out. "You won't tell anyone that I was hoping for a message from Waddler, will you? I mean, I feel so ashamed that I didn't even pray. Oh, Faith, what can I do? I've been spending all my time on my outside beauty and not on the things that would make me beautiful inside—like keeping my promise to Waddler to pray. And when I got Waddler's message, I felt more ashamed than ever." She looked over at her miserably.

"I've never really thought about beauty being 'outside or inside,' but now that you mention it, it's true. It's inside beauty that matters to The Maker . . . and to Waddler, too, I think." As Faith spoke, she noticed that Posie's gaze had wandered to her reflection.

An awkward silence made Posie aware of her action. She looked up in embarrassment. "Oh, Faith, it's as if I'm chained to my reflection, and I wish I weren't! If only I had never looked!"

"Well, you can stop," said Faith matter-of-factly.

Posie stared at her for a long while and then hung her head sadly. "But that's just it," she admitted, "I even promised myself and The Maker that I would pray for Waddler, and instead . . ."

"Well, I'll help you stop," announced Faith with determination. She got up and motioned for Posie to follow, and together, they left the brook and the reflecting pool behind. They walked along silently at first, and then Faith suggested, "Why don't we pray for Waddler and the others now, while we're walking?"

They had never walked and prayed at the same time before, but the two found that it was a good use of their time. Before long they were almost home. Then they chatted together like old friends.

Faith explained what Seeker had translated that very day at breakfast. "The highway of the Upright is to depart from evil."

"That's what I need to do, Faith, and you've helped me do it. It's not that the reflecting pool is evil, but when I spend my time looking at my reflection instead of praying, that *is* evil of me, and I need to depart from it," she reasoned aloud.

"Well, I'll help you stay on the highway of the Upright."

"How?" Posie stopped and turned toward Faith, puzzled.

"From now on, *I'll* go and get the messages. You can wait for me here on the pathway, and we'll pray for the boys all the

way to the clinic and back! And let's call this path the Highway of the Upright!" They both giggled about their new secret name.

Later that day, when Posie and Faith came home, they had cobwebs hanging from their ears and clumps of dirt between their toes, but it didn't matter to either of them. They felt much happier about their inward appearance. They had kept their promise to pray.

Upright
*B*efore the Maker

*I was also Upright before him, and I kept
myself from mine iniquity.*
Psalm 18:23

POSIE WAS intently watching Aunt Serenity prepare a
breakfast of dried berries. She was sorting through the
pile of berries carefully, discarding leaves and dirt that
had gotten mixed in. To Posie, who now noticed appearances,
Aunt Serenity looked very beautiful. It wasn't her fur, because
for as long as Posie could remember, it had been faded and
shaggy. Her whiskers drooped with age, and the dirt, once on
the berries, now covered her paws. And yet with all of these
defects, an unmistakable beauty shone through, leaving Posie
very perplexed. *Where does beauty come from?* she wondered to
herself.

She watched Aunt Serenity dip the berries one by one into a
shell of clean water. And then, a little embarrassed, she asked,
"Aunt Serenity, how did you get to be beautiful?"

Aunt Serenity smiled, amused at the question, but then seeing
Posie was serious, she grew quiet and thought for a moment.
Then she shrugged and said, "It's never been awful important to
me, Little Flower. Y'see, I've never thought of bein' beautiful—
'ceptin' to The Maker."

Posie leaned forward. It was always this way with adults.
They could never speak plainly. You always had to make your
own sense out of what they said. She probed further. "But *how*
do you become beautiful to The Maker?"

"Well, I s'pose iffen I am, it's by walkin' Uprightly before Him and keepin' my heart from badness."

So that was her secret! At last Posie knew how to become beautiful, but to check her conclusions, she asked, "Aunt Serenity, if I walk Uprightly before The Maker and keep my heart from badness, will I become beautiful too?"

Aunt Serenity

"To The Maker you will, Little Flower. And though I've never really thought of it, maybe to others too. But pleasin' The Maker is the most important thing of all."

"Oh, I will, Aunt Serenity!" promised Posie, and she meant it with all her heart.

Almost immediately, she devised a plan that she secretly called "Pleasing The Maker First." Knowing that it began with doing her job, Posie made a list of all the things she was expected to do. Then she quietly did them without being told. And so it was that at supper time, shells mysteriously appeared on the rock table ahead of schedule, fresh fir needles were gathered each day for their beds, and even the floors were swept daily. No one seemed to notice her doing it, and at first no one even commented. Posie wondered if anyone cared, but she continued doing her jobs.

Daily, she and Faith made trips to the clinic to visit their little patient. They had named her Joy because, as they said, it was a joy to take care of her. Even Stealer, who sometimes filled in for them when they were gone, seemed to enjoy caring for the little patient. And all the way to the clinic and back, Posie and Faith made good use of their time by praying for their four missionaries far away in foreign countries.

Posie worked hard at pleasing The Maker. While at first she was disappointed that no one seemed to notice, she was sure that The Maker did, and she cared only about being beautiful in His eyes. And so, no longer did she visit the reflecting pool. Instead she could usually be found at the clinic holding Joy and taking her for short walks, or at home teaching Furry-Ball and Sunshine from The Book. In fact, she got so much enjoyment from her new plan to please The Maker first that she began to look for ways to do even more. And it was then that the family began to notice.

"You're a mighty fine example to us all, Little Flower," said Seeker one day, beaming with pride. He had just been sampling her recently invented dried berry and acorn stew.

Posie blushed. (Although blushing has rarely been observed in raccoons!) And for once she had nothing to say.

Several more weeks went by, and Posie's acts of kindness continued. Soon her kindness became contagious, and the whole family was involved in a war of kindness—each one outdoing the other. Cross words were hardly ever exchanged, and more work than ever got done. Even their enemies benefited from the overflow of kindness, and that was especially true at the clinic.

And so it was that on a cold and threatening day, though spring was just around the corner, Posie and Faith were on their way to the clinic. They had stopped along the pathway, and Faith had turned off toward the brook to check for messages while Posie waited.

Moments later Faith came running toward her. In between breaths she blurted out, "Waddler and Trasher are returning soon!" She held out the piece of bark still dripping with water.

Posie trembled with excitement as she read the message for herself, and for the first time in many days, she wondered if Waddler would notice her when he returned. Perhaps she would have gone back to her old ways of thinking had not something happened right then. A snowflake fell, and it brought them both back to the present—their trip to the clinic.

"Oh, no!" gasped Faith. "If the snow falls fast, Stealer will be stranded with little Joy, and they have no food. But if we both go to the clinic, the others won't get the message from Waddler and Trasher! What shall we do?" She looked at Posie in bewilderment.

"I'll take the food to the clinic, and you go back and tell the others," Posie said decisively. Then, gathering up the bundle of food, she turned and was gone before Faith could even protest.

The snow fell thick and fast as Posie hurried on her mission, but she concentrated on doing her job—she had to! Stealer and Joy were depending on her! But by the time she got halfway there, the snow was so deep that it became increasingly difficult to walk or even see the path.

"Please help me, Dear Maker," she prayed aloud more than once. And He did. Almost at the point of exhaustion, she dragged

herself to within sight of the clinic and staggered the last few steps to the doorway.

Stealer helped her into the warmth and safety of the cozy room and quickly arranged a soft bed of dry fir needles. Her teeth were still chattering as she explained the reason why she was alone.

Stealer was very touched. Never had anyone showed such kindness to him before. "You risked your life in coming," he said quietly.

"It was the least I could do," Posie responded, breaking open the bundle of food.

And then an amazing conversation followed—one that would never have happened had not Posie been pleasing The Maker first. Stealer told Posie the story of his life—how he had been abandoned as a youngster and had been on his own ever since.

At last Posie understood why Stealer was so attached to little Joy—his life had begun much like hers. That was the reason why he could not bear to see her abandoned. How amazing that The

Maker would bring Stealer into their lives through this little baby! Posie thought about this as she listened to his story.

Then at last Stealer began to ask her questions—questions like, "What makes you so kind?" and "How do you know The Maker cares about me?" In fact, for the first time since they had met him, Stealer was open to hearing about The Maker, and when the conversation ended, he told her that he wanted to hear more.

Posie fell asleep at last, and as she slept, she dreamed about Methuselah and Aunt Serenity. To her, they were both very beautiful. What she didn't see was that she was also becoming beautiful.

CHAPTER 18

Kept Safe

He is a shield to those who walk Uprightly.
Proverbs 2:7

THE SNOW continued all the next day. Night had fallen, and the storm was still howling outside.

"Without more food, we'll all die," Stealer said, defending his decision to Posie.

Against Posie's advice, Stealer had decided to go for help. He knew the way, he assured her, and had the strength to make the trip. Without further argument, he departed, leaving Posie behind with Joy. She spent a sleepless night, but prayed much for Stealer.

When daylight broke, it seemed to Posie that the storm had increased in fury. The wind blew so hard that the coziness of the room had been replaced by a chill and draftiness that sent shivers down her spine. By noon, the last of the food was gone, and still Stealer had not come back. Posie was concerned. What if something had happened to him? That thought finally led her to a decision—she would take Joy with her and return to the family. She would look for Stealer along the way.

Bundling leaves tightly around Joy, she left the shelter of the clinic and started out. Bitter wind tore at her face, and even her thick fur could not keep out the cold dampness of the snow. Bending her body into the wind, she moved forward, praying for strength as she went.

Several hours passed, and still she had not seen Stealer. By her estimation, she was less than halfway home, and her strength was running out. Ahead loomed the darkness of an overhanging bough. Stooping down, she crept under its shelter, thankful that the heavy bough shielded her from the wind and snow. Then gently sliding Joy off her back, she felt her tiny body. It was very cold so Posie put her arms around her and pulled her to her own body to warm her. When at last she heard a little whimper, she breathed a sigh of relief.

But then a feeling of despair followed, and Posie began to cry. It wasn't for herself that she cried—it was for this tiny little baby whose life was threatened once more. Suddenly, her own life meant nothing to her compared to the life of this little one. She was beginning to understand why Methuselah gave his life for Rabid, and why The Maker gave His life for His lost Uprights. Surely, The Maker cared about this precious life. If only He would bring someone to help her.

Posie knew that time was running out. She felt so cold that she could no longer cry. Determined to give the last of her warmth to little Joy, she covered her with her body and would have fallen asleep had not her imagination played a trick on her. She thought that she heard someone calling her.

"Posie! POSIE!"

"I did hear someone!" she said aloud. "The Maker did send someone! I'M HERE!" she yelled, but her voice could barely be heard above the noise of the wind.

Yet footsteps came nearer and nearer, and then the bough snapped as someone lifted it. Waddler stepped in and stood for a moment as his eyes adjusted to the darkness. "Posie!" he exclaimed, and bending down, he felt her fur. "You're so cold!" He took her paw in his own and then saw little Joy.

"Help her first," whispered Posie weakly.

Waddler leaned out of the shelter. "Over here, Trasher!"

Within seconds, the two were lifting Posie and Joy onto their makeshift sled (the Upright-mover turned upside down). Posie managed to smile at their resourcefulness. Covering both with dry leaves, they set out, pulling the sled forward as fast as they could.

They were almost home when Joy warmed up enough to whimper again. Posie felt hungry and cold herself, but most of all, she felt a sense of gratitude to The Maker for the help He sent. "Praise The Maker for sending you!" she called out.

"Praise is especially beautiful on you!" yelled back Waddler as he turned with a smile.

Posie felt warm all over at his words. She knew that he couldn't possibly be talking about how she looked. And yet, she felt warmer still to think that perhaps, to The Maker, she was beautiful because she had pleased Him first.

At last they were home, and there sitting in the middle of the family circle was Stealer. It was his return that had prompted Waddler and Trasher, who had just returned themselves, to leave the comfort of their warm home and help Posie and Joy. Face to face with each other again, Posie and Stealer could only smile in relief that their terrible ordeal was over and Joy was safe.

Tidy-Paw and Aunt Serenity brought out shells heaped with food, and it was all quickly devoured. Faith coaxed some food into Joy and then tucked her into a warm bed. The coziness of the room soon warmed the rest of them, and before long, conversation and laughter flowed. Waddler and Trasher recounted many of their adventures, including how they had learned the language of the foreign raccoons.

Seeker then translated from The Book. "He is a shield to those who walk Uprightly." A quietness came over them all as they thought about the truth of these words. Then Seeker prayed for Puddly and Truster, who were still away, and the others prayed along with him. Later, while Tidy-Paw and Aunt Serenity were tucking the two littlest raccoons into their beds, Stealer took the opportunity to talk with Seeker and Rapid about The Maker.

At last the storm stopped, and the moon shone brightly on the snow. Waddler whispered quietly to Faith, Posie, and Trasher, "Now that we're all rested and warm, why don't we go sledding? We can use the Upright-mover! The moon is so bright that it'll be absolutely safe!"

They tiptoed out. Moonbeams danced on the snow, magically sprinkling the whole forest with diamonds. The four friends chatted back and forth merrily as they climbed the hill, then by pairs, slid down. And that is how it was that Posie found herself climbing up the hill with Waddler. The snow crunched underfoot, and the moon's reflection made even their fur sparkle.

"Posie," he began shyly, "you are very dear to me." He stopped and faced her. "Today when I found you almost frozen with cold, I realized that part of my heart would die if anything happened to you. When I saw how you were trying to give the last of your warmth to little Joy, you seemed very beautiful to me." He smiled at her.

She smiled back shyly. "It was all I could do," she said. Then holding on tightly, they slid down the hill together.

CHAPTER 19

Growing Pains

The tent of the Upright will flourish.
Proverbs 14:11

AN EARLY spring thaw had melted the snow, but another kind of thaw had taken place too. After his long
talk with Seeker the night of the blizzard, Stealer's cold
heart had melted, and he had decided to follow The Maker. And,
like Rapid, he was a changed raccoon. Oh, he still had a rough
veneer, but deep down inside, the toughness was gone, and there
was a gentleness about him. It showed especially with Joy, who
more and more began to bond with him. Sometimes she mistak-
enly called him "Daddy," and though he seemed embarrassed at
first, he gradually became more used to it and was clearly pleased
that she had "adopted" him. And being an adopted father, not
only was he concerned to learn all that he could about The Maker,
but he insisted that Posie and Faith include Joy in their teaching
about The Maker.

After one of these teaching sessions, they felt that the little
ones needed a break from their lessons and decided to go out.
The adults were deeply engrossed in discussion and translation
work, and they were only too happy to have a few quiet moments
without the noise. Posie and Faith headed down to the brook
overflow with the three littlest raccoons and the Upright-mover.
Though much of the snow had melted, it was still rather nippy
out, and they were hoping that the ice on the overflow would be
thick enough for gliding. Sure enough, they found that conditions

couldn't have been more perfect. For the most part, the ice seemed thick and smooth. Furry-Ball and Sunshine were delighted to be out in the fresh air again. They began to play crack the whip and tag, and raced from one end of the overflow to the other, leaving little Joy far behind.

"Wait for me!" she called out time and again, but often they did not even hear her. Posie and Faith watched, encouraging her to catch up, and making sure that she did not venture near thin ice.

They were happily gliding back and forth when Posie suddenly stopped and turned to Faith. Half whispering, she said, "There it is again! That face behind the bush over there! It's gone now, but I'm sure I saw it!"

"I saw it too," said Faith, a worried look on her face. "I wonder who she is."

"I don't know, but we seem to see her every time we take Joy out. And Stealer seems to know her. Have you noticed how uneasy he gets when we see her?"

"I feel uneasy too," admitted Faith. "She looks like she's up to no good. Do you think she's trying to kidnap little Joy?" Nervously, they hurried toward Joy, who at that very moment was gliding toward the opposite side of the overflow, totally unaware of any danger. In seconds she would be within reach of that hidden stranger.

"Joy, stop!" Posie called out in alarm. Joy turned and obeyed instantly.

"Come here!" shouted Faith, relieved when Joy turned to come. But as she obeyed, a dark raccoon figure crept out from behind the bush and stealthily made her way to the overflow edge. Posie and Faith froze in horror as the stranger moved out on the ice toward Joy. Then, just as she was within reach of Joy's tail, a terrifying noise filled the air and echoed the whole length of the overflow.

CRRRRRAAAAAACK!

Filled with fear, Posie and Faith ran forward to grab Joy, pulling her to safety just seconds before the ice where she had stood disappeared beneath the water. Next they looked for Sunshine and Furry-Ball. To their relief, they saw them running toward them, waving their arms.

"She's gone!" they yelled, pointing to the ice.

It was true. A huge gaping hole was all that remained where the dark figure had last been seen. And then a paw reached up out of that hole and grasped for the edge of the ice. But just as quickly, it disappeared again into the cold dark water.

Never one to ignore suffering, Posie was propelled into action by her pity for the stranger. Creeping out carefully but swiftly toward the hole, she lay on her stomach and approached the edge inch by inch. The paw reached up out of the hole again, and Posie stretched for it, but missed, and almost slid into the hole.

Faith, seeing this, took immediate action. She ordered Sunshine to stay behind with Joy, and then motioned for Furry to follow her. Together, careful not to increase the size of the crack, they slowly edged their way out toward Posie. Flattening themselves on the ice, they linked tail and paw to make a chain.

At that point Sunshine had an idea. Practically pulling Joy through the air, he sped home for help, and as he entered the clearing, he blurted out the news, "Hurry! A stranger's fallen through the ice, and we can't get her out!"

Waddler and Trasher raced after him, getting the story from Sunshine as they ran. At last they reached the edge of the overflow, and as they did so, their eyes quickly took in the desperate scene. They saw a paw reaching frantically for the edge of the ice. Then, though Posie strained to grab hold of the stranger, she disappeared again into the blackness.

Trasher sized up the situation quickly. "Follow me!" he called to Waddler as he grabbed a long stick from the edge of the overflow. Seeing that Posie was in imminent danger, he quietly, but firmly, ordered her to move back. Then, stretching the stick into the hole, he lay on his stomach. Waddler did the same and

held fast to Trasher's foot. The other raccoons continued the chain until Furry's tail reached the edge where Sunshine held on to him.

They waited for what seemed like hours, almost fearing that it was too late, when at last the paw reached up one more time. It would have disappeared forever had not Trasher pushed the stick down into the water in the direction of that dark shape. But at last the paw grabbed onto the stick, and the tug was felt all the way to Sunshine at the edge of the overflow. It took all of them together, straining their hardest, to pull the stranger out, but in the end, they accomplished their mission.

"We have no time to lose!" yelled Waddler as they carried the limp form of the stranger to safety. Then Posie and Faith took over. It seemed odd to be working so hard to save the life of this stranger, who minutes before had tried to kidnap Joy. But work they did, and none too soon—she had swallowed a great deal of water, and she was very cold. They lifted her onto the Upright-mover, covered her with dry leaves, and then took her home. There, Tidy-Paw and Aunt Serenity attended to her until at last she stirred.

Opening her eyes, she whispered, "I'm sorry for all the trouble. I changed my mind . . . and I just wanted her back." Her eyes closed again.

Posie looked over at Stealer. His eyes were wide with fear. "Who is she, Stealer?" she probed.

Stealer looked at her in sadness. "She's Joy's mother," he confessed at last. "I saw her when she abandoned her baby."

Honor

They gasped. At first it was the shock of knowing the hideous truth about this stranger. Here was a mother who had left her baby to die. But then pity for her welled up in their hearts, because they realized that even though she didn't know The Maker, she had seen the error of her way and now wanted her baby back.

The mother stirred again and tried to sit up. "I know I don't deserve her," she stammered weakly. "I don't know what made me do it. But it's all right if you keep her. You've cared for her. I've seen you with my own eyes. But I don't understand why. You didn't have to do it." Exhausted, she closed her eyes and fell back again.

Seeker motioned for them to let her sleep. Then, as a family, they drew apart in another corner and prayed, asking The Maker to heal her.

As they finished praying, Stealer sighed. "If she decides to follow The Maker, I don't see why we shouldn't give her baby back." A tear rolled down his cheek.

It was just at that moment that Joy, who had been playing with Sunshine and Furry-Ball, came over and climbed up on Stealer's lap. "Don't cry, Daddy," she said.

Soon they were all crying—all except Joy, who did not understand what was happening. And as they cried, they realized why they were crying—it wasn't always easy to do The Maker's will. They all agreed with Stealer, but knew that if they had to give her back, they'd miss this tiny one whom they had come to love so much.

Their prayers were answered several days later, however, when with the encouragement of Tidy-Paw and Aunt Serenity, Joy's mother decided to follow The Maker. Her decision was real, and it was obvious to them all that she had changed. She stayed for many days with them, learning about The Maker and watching her little daughter from a distance. Several times the family saw Stealer and Honor (as they now called Joy's mother) talking together, but nothing could have prepared them for the exciting news that followed.

One day Stealer made an announcement. Clearing his throat to get their attention, he began: "A while back we all agreed that if Honor decided to follow The Maker, we would return her daughter to her. As you know, she has become a follower. And what's more, she decided to follow The Maker without even knowing about our decision. She's an honor to The Maker, and I think we ought to honor our decision." Stealer's announcement came as a surprise, and they hung their heads sadly. Stealer cleared his throat again. A broad smile spread across his face. "But not before we make another announcement!" He looked over at Honor. She smiled back shyly and took his paw. "Honor and I would like to announce our engagement!"

Posie's eyes widened. "Is it true?" she squealed in delight. The smiles on the faces of Stealer and Honor told her all that she needed to know. Then, overcome with happiness, she hugged them both, and soon the entire family was hugging and embracing one another. Their eyes shone with tears—but this time they were tears of joy.

"This calls for a celebration!" exclaimed Aunt Serenity. "It's not every day we have an engagement!"

And what a celebration they had! There were special treats and games and singing. They even had a ceremony in which they officially changed Stealer's name to Giver and pronounced them engaged. And at dark, they all raced to the ice for a gliding party. The moon shone brightly as the happy group laughed and played together. Out of breath, Waddler and Posie glided over to an old log and sat down to rest.

"It's really worth it to follow The Maker, Waddler," Posie was saying. "It seems that even when sad things happen, He changes them into happy things!"

"It *is* strange," Waddler admitted. He looked over at the dark hole where Honor had disappeared. "You might say that without sadness, the good things wouldn't have happened. The Maker certainly proved that with Honor and Stealer. . . . I mean Giver," Waddler corrected himself. "And now there are more followers of The Maker than ever in our land."

He looked down at Posie listening intently to his every word. The moonlight glistened on her fur and sparkled in her black eyes. Waddler thought she had never looked so beautiful, and yet

it wasn't only what she looked like that attracted him. It was all that she was—kind and unselfish, sympathetic and, most of all, the way she loved The Maker.

Suddenly, Waddler could control himself no longer. He took her by the paw and pulled her out onto the ice and whirled her around and around until she was breathless and dizzy.

When at last they both collapsed in a heap laughing, all Posie could say was, "Oh, Waddler!"

CHAPTER 20

*L*Faithful in *L*ittle Things

A faithful God who does no wrong,
Upright and just is he.
Deuteronomy 32:4

IT JUST wasn't fair! Furry-Ball hadn't planned on being angry, but this was just too much. He and Sunshine were tagging along behind Posie and Faith, and he was sulking as he went.
"What's wrong, Furry?" questioned Sunshine at last.

"Everything!" muttered Furry-Ball, kicking a pebble as he went. He just didn't want to talk about it. Down deep, he knew it was wrong to be angry about his problem, yet he just couldn't help himself. Hoping Sunshine wouldn't probe, he walked along silently.

"Everything?" repeated Sunshine.

Furry-Ball wished he could ignore him, but he could tell that Sunshine was not going to go away. "For one thing, *THIS!*" he said indignantly, pointing to their sisters up ahead.

"I don't get it." Sunshine was looking at Furry with a very puzzled expression.

"Tell me something, Sunshine, did you hear what Father read from The Book this morning?"

"Well, yes . . . that The Maker was Upright and just."

"Well, do you think it's fair that Waddler and Trasher and Puddly and Truster get to be missionaries and we don't?"

"Yes, but Waddler told us it was just as important to stay behind and pray, remember?"

"That's girl stuff!" Furry-Ball said irreverently. "And so is this!" he said again, pointing to the two up ahead. "All we ever get to do is stay with the girls. No one ever asks us to do anything dangerous like being missionaries. We just get stuck here all the time treated like girls."

"Furry, you're just having a bad day," Sunshine said patiently, trying to understand why Furry-Ball was so grouchy.

Furry-Ball stopped. Looking Sunshine right in the eye, he continued ranting. "Think about it, Sunshine. Even Rapid and Giver get to go and preach to the bandits, and where are we? Here with the girls, that's where! And what are we doing? Going to see an Upright wedding, that's what," he said in a mocking syrupy-sweet voice. "And if that isn't girl stuff, what is?"

"I s'pose you're right, Furry. I've never really thought about it like that." He frowned. "Maybe we should talk to Father about it. He probably doesn't realize we're old enough now to get away from these girls and do dangerous stuff."

"Furry! Sunshine!" called Posie from far ahead. "Hurry or we'll be late!"

Furry-Ball glanced angrily toward them and in a high mocking voice said, so that only Sunshine could hear him, "Huuurrry or we'll be late!"

"Come on, Furry. We'll get in trouble if we argue with the girls. Let's just go with them this time, and then we can talk to Father. And maybe we can get Waddler on our side too."

They raced ahead to join Faith and Posie, who were already at the wall by the Big House. Furry-Ball felt better. He didn't know why, but somehow, talking about it to Sunshine made him think that the problem would be solved and that they wouldn't be stuck for the rest of their lives following their sisters around. Yet, still feeling a tiny bit argumentative, when they had caught up with Posie and Faith, Furry-Ball raised a question: "How do you know that the Uprights are having a wedding right now, and who wants to go to an old wedding anyhow?"

"You know the silver treasure chest behind the Big House, Furry? Well, we translated the announcement on a leaf we found there! And besides, we need to learn about weddings so that we can do the wedding right for Giver and Honor." Posie, who had not heard her brothers' conversation about girl stuff, seemed hurt at Furry-Ball's challenge.

Sunshine shot Furry a warning glance. Reluctantly, they followed Posie and Faith over the wall and toward the Big House. Strange sounds coming from the clear stone openings told them that their sisters were probably right—there was an Upright Gathering of some sort taking place.

"See!" Posie said to Furry-Ball reprovingly. Then, motioning for the others to join her in forming a raccoon platform, she directed Furry to stand on top of their backs and look through the clear stone opening. This done, she pressed him for news. "Well, what do you see, Furry?"

"You're right!" he said at last as he stared through the opening in amazement. "This *is* a wedding!"

"Tell us what you see!" urged Faith.

"I've never seen so many Uprights since the time when I was trapped inside the Big House!" he reported. "They're all dressed funny, and it looks like they're all waiting for something to happen." He paused. "And now something *is!*"

That was all Posie had to hear. She yanked Furry down and climbed up herself. She stood there just long enough to see Sarah, along with some bigger Uprights, walking down the aisle holding a beautiful bouquet of flowers, when all of a sudden, the raccoon platform lost its balance and toppled her to the ground. "I'm sorry," she apologized. "I just had to see. Please forgive me, Furry. You're lighter. Would you climb up again and tell us what's happening?"

Furry-Ball hesitated for a moment, but curiosity got the better of him, and he climbed up obediently. Though inwardly he was very interested in what he saw, his report came out with only

the barest details. "They're standing in front of an Upright who's reading from what looks like The Book," he said mechanically.

"Who, Furry? Who's standing in front?" Faith asked.

"Them. They are, that's who," he answered dully. Then, for the second time, he felt himself being yanked down, and this time it was Faith who took his place.

"Oooohhhh!" was all that she could report before the platform again came tumbling down.

It was a long time before they could convince Furry-Ball to climb up again, and when they did, he had even less to report, though that was partly because of what he saw. If you've ever seen something that was so embarrassing that it left you speechless, you know how Furry-Ball felt. The wedding was almost over when he saw the woman Upright and the man Upright turn to each other, and then, bending their heads slightly, they . . . Furry could not believe his eyes! Partly out of shock and partly out of disgust, he covered his eyes with his paw. And though the others pressed him to tell them, he would never reveal what he saw (though he never forgot it!).

They were on their way home at last. Furry-Ball and Sunshine, who were not at all interested in the girls' "wedding talk," once again lagged behind. They were imagining what it would be like to go on dangerous missions when a loud snap came from the direction of the brook.

"It's him!" whispered Furry-Ball hoarsely. He pointed to the familiar shape of an Upright boy walking at the brook's edge. "He's the one who set the trap for Waddler. I still hate him!" he muttered.

They watched him quietly. Then Sunshine spoke. "Waddler said it's because he doesn't go into the Big House—that's why he's mean. I wonder if we could ever get him to go in," he said wistfully, and then he sighed.

"He'll never go in," responded Furry-Ball flatly.

"You never know, Furry," was all that Sunshine said, and then they slipped away quietly.

Later, after arriving home, they sought out Seeker. With much complaining, they poured out their hearts about always "getting stuck with girl stuff," and then waited for his response. But instead of assigning them to a dangerous mission, Seeker encouraged them to continue serving The Maker in small ways—even if it meant being with their sisters.

"I just translated an important document," Seeker told them. They leaned forward in interest. "In The Book it says that 'he who is faithful in a very little thing is faithful also in much.' You see, The Maker Himself is faithful, and He expects us to be faithful, too—even if it seems like a little thing."

Furry-Ball couldn't really argue with that. In his heart, he knew that The Maker *was* fair, and he began to feel ashamed of himself for thinking otherwise. But he still wasn't happy about always "getting stuck following his sisters around."

Later, along with Sunshine, he tried to explain his feelings to Waddler. "It's not that I don't like the girls. It's just that they don't ever do anything interesting. They're always picking flowers instead of doing dangerous things like going on missionary trips."

"I can understand how you feel, Furry, but Father was right when he told you to be faithful in the little things first." Furry-

Ball and Sunshine hung their heads. "But that is not to say you can't find dangerous things to do right here at home as you serve The Maker." At this remark, they perked right up.

"What do you mean, Waddler?" asked Furry-Ball excitedly.

"I mean that if you keep your eyes open, you'll find lots of opportunities to serve The Maker, and some may even be dangerous. It seems to me that you're so busy complaining about what you can't be doing that you don't appreciate what you *can* be doing."

"I guess it's true," admitted Furry-Ball when he and Sunshine were alone. "But what is there to do that's dangerous?"

They were walking very near the brook at this point when something glistened through the branches. Furry-Ball pulled a branch aside and peered through. Pointing to a trap across the brook, he said, "He's up to his old tricks again."

Sunshine sighed. "Now *this* would be dangerous."

"You mean springing the trap?"

"No, I mean trying to get that Upright to go into the Big House," answered Sunshine. "Springing the trap would be dangerous, but it wouldn't stop him. He'd probably just set another one. We've got to think of a way to get him into the Big House."

"You're right," agreed Furry-Ball, "because if he came to know The Maker, then maybe he'd stop setting traps."

Furry-Ball and Sunshine talked for a long time. They had to find a way to accomplish this dangerous mission. Furry-Ball suggested that together maybe they could chase him in, but Sunshine dismissed this plan entirely.

"He might not stay inside long enough for The Maker to change him," he argued.

They went back and forth with their plans—first one thing and then another. By this time they had reached the wall. They

peered over and sighed, each wishing secretly that they would see their enemy Upright go into the Big House. They watched for a while, but no one came. By now it was getting near supper time, and their noses picked up the delicious scent of food coming from the silver treasure chest behind the Big House. Together, they darted over to the chest, and within seconds, Furry's nimble fingers had pried off the lid, and the two were inside exploring the contents.

"Do you see this?" Sunshine exclaimed as he held a delectable piece of sugar-frosted food in his paw. "And look, here's more! It must be what the bandits call wedding food!"

The two stuffed themselves, but try as they might, for once, they could not eat it all. They were about to leave much of the food behind when Sunshine came up with an idea. "Why not take some of this home," he suggested, "and give it to our enemies when they come to the Gatherings?"

Furry-Ball agreed. Tearing leaves from an old book that had no cover, they wrapped each piece and stored the food in a temporary hiding place nearby. They were almost finished when Furry noticed one of the leaves. "Look, Sunshine! These leaves are from The Book!" His face fell. "We didn't recognize it because there was no hard leaf on the outside. I'm sure glad it's not *our* Book, but it's definitely The Book, all right. If only we had known . . . we would never have . . ." his voice trailed off.

The damage was done. They had torn out the pages, and there was no way to put them back. Furry-Ball and Sunshine felt very bad for destroying The Book, yet they knew they hadn't meant to do this terrible thing. They picked up the remaining section and were just about to go when Furry-Ball had an idea.

"Since we've already torn some leaves out, why not tear out more and put them by the trap? Maybe the Upright will read them and decide to follow The Maker!"

Eagerly rushing to the brook, they carefully placed some leaves from The Book as close to that dangerous object as they dared. Then, hiding the rest of their treasure in a safe place, they raced home, barely making it in time for supper.

As for supper, they hardly ate any of it and said little about where they had been. Too much wedding food had spoiled their appetites. But not their excitement. Their minds were whirling 'round and 'round with the things that they had accomplished that afternoon. Furry-Ball and Sunshine had to agree with Waddler—it was amazing how dangerous it could be right in your own backyard when you kept your eyes open and were faithful in the little things.

CHAPTER 21

ecrets

Such as are blameless in their ways
are His delight.
Proverbs 11:20

I
T WAS one of those mornings that called to you to get up and get going. Birds sang as if it were the first day of spring. Warm breezes blew gently through the evergreen boughs, and yellow-green grass poked its way upward in the midst of last year's pale dried stalks. Most probably winter would have one last fling, but for this morning, the whole family was up and busy, intent on enjoying every minute of this beautiful day.

Furry-Ball and Sunshine had a secret, and as they followed their sisters that morning, their mission took on added excitement. They planned to check the trap (secretly, of course), and they were sure that the Upright had found the leaves from The Book.

They lagged just far enough behind to be able to talk privately, and had gone along for quite some time without saying anything when Furry-Ball finally spoke. "I'm really sorry, Sunshine, for saying that The Maker wasn't fair. Father's right. We need to be faithful in little things before we can be trusted in big things."

"Oh, I understand, Furry. Sometimes it does seem a little boring always following the girls. But not since we've been keeping our eyes open. In fact, it's getting mighty dangerous lately!"

Furry-Ball nodded in agreement. He was quiet for a while, and then he spoke again. "Most of all," he said, "I want The Maker to be proud of me."

"Me too," answered Sunshine, and his eyes shone with determination.

Just then they heard Faith up ahead shouting. "Hurry, boys," she called. "We've got to get all these invitations delivered before it's too late. After all, the wedding's tomorrow!"

(Although no one has yet been able to decipher the written language of raccoons, everyone who has ever spent any time in the forest knows that they regularly send "letters" back and forth to each other. This is how strangers passing through know what back porch, patio, or deck to visit to obtain a free meal. Humans don't often recognize these letters, but once every hundred years or so, one does come to light. Posie and Faith's invitations were just such letters.)

"If only Needlenose would come!" Posie was saying as Furry-Ball and Sunshine caught up with her at last. She sighed. "He used to be one of Giver's best friends. It's a shame he's never come to our Gatherings."

Hearing that remark, Furry-Ball and Sunshine exchanged glances. Then in lowered tones, Furry-Ball said, "There's only one way that Needlenose would ever come."

"What's that, Furry?"

"Free food. He'll do anything for food."

"Who told you that?" Sunshine asked.

"Giver," he answered matter-of-factly. "And he ought to know."

"Well, we have some food that we could donate. Remember?"

Furry-Ball could remember only too well. He could almost taste it in his mouth. In fact, he had been counting the minutes until they got to the place where the food was hidden. "I s'pose we *could* share," he offered grudgingly.

"It does seem like the Upright thing to do," Sunshine responded, though his voice totally lacked enthusiasm. "But how do we go about doing it?"

A gurgling sound interrupted their conversation. They had rounded the bend, and the brook lay just ahead. Checking carefully to see that their sisters weren't watching, Furry-Ball and Sunshine pulled the boughs aside and slipped furtively down to the water's edge. There, not too far away, was the dreaded trap, but their eyes scanned the scene for something else.

"They're gone!" yelled Furry-Ball. And so they were. There was no trace of the white leaves they had left the day before.

"Look!" added Sunshine. "He was here all right. Here are his tracks!"

Quickly, they made their way back to the path, and when Posie and Faith called next, it was clear they had not even missed the two adventurers on their detour to the brook.

"Let's get some more leaves," whispered Sunshine secretly. "Maybe if he reads more, he'll follow The Maker."

"It seems to be working so far," said Furry-Ball encouragingly. Then he grew quiet, and after a few moments he said, "You know, I've been thinking. If we could get the Upright to read about The Maker simply by sharing the leaves from The Book

we found, maybe we *could* get Needlenose and his friends to come to the wedding by sharing our food. Then they would hear about The Maker, because Father plans to talk from The Book, you know."

"But how will they know about the food?" asked Sunshine.

"We'll leave them a little sample," answered Furry-Ball. "And then we'll promise them more if they come."

"That's a great idea, Furry!" Sunshine beamed from ear to ear. "But how will we promise them more?" His smile vanished.

"We'll watch carefully where the girls leave the invitations and go back later. Then we'll add our promise to their invitation and leave a sample of the food," he said confidently.

"And we can't forget to get more leaves from The Book for the Upright," added Sunshine.

It was settled. And now all they needed was the time to accomplish their secret mission. That moment arrived several hours later when, after all the invitations had been left, Posie announced a break and sat down to eat lunch.

"If only we could find golden bands like I saw in the Upright wedding," Faith was saying. "The Uprights gave them to each other," she added dreamily.

"What do you think the bands meant?" asked Posie curiously.

She leaned toward Posie. "I'm sure they meant, 'I love you!'" she whispered.

Furry-Ball overheard this, and it was more than he could bear. He looked over at Sunshine with disgust and beckoned for him to follow. Then, turning to leave, he shouted over his shoulder, "We'll be back."

"Where are you going?" Faith called. "Don't you want lunch?"

"It's a secret," answered Furry-Ball smugly. "But we won't be too long," he promised.

Then, hurrying toward the hidden food, they helped themselves to quite large portions, and gathering as much as they could carry, they retraced their footsteps. By each invitation they left a small sample and added these words, written in mud, "More food if you come." They left a particularly large sample by Needlenose's invitation. Then, that part of their mission complete, they hurried back to the brook. There they tore out more leaves from The Book and carefully left them by the trap.

"We'd better go back now," Sunshine said when they had finished.

When they returned, to their surprise, only Faith was there. She was talking with Trasher who had just arrived, and she was weaving a small straw ring. She tried it on as she talked.

"It means, 'I love you,'" she was explaining. "I saw it in the Upright wedding."

Furry-Ball turned away again, in disgust. Even Sunshine was listening intently, he noticed, and suddenly, he felt almost sick to his stomach. Wandering toward a sunny meadow alone, he spied Posie's wreath, just visible above a clump of tall grass. He had come from behind and was just about to call out to her when he heard her speak.

"Maybe he does, or maybe he doesn't," she was saying in a singsongy voice. At the same time she was pulling petals off a small white flower.

Furry-Ball immediately recognized what she was doing. (Now while it is true that Uprights practice a similar tradition of pulling petals from a daisy while saying, "He loves me. He loves me not," some people believe that the true origin of this tradition can be traced back to raccoons.) Again Furry-Ball turned on his heels in disgust and climbed up a steep rock pile behind Posie. Since she was facing away from him, he was convinced that he was totally hidden from view. He watched her carefully. Although he wanted to get far away from all this "love stuff," it seemed to be everywhere. Yet, at the same time, he was very intrigued and could not stop watching. And this is what he saw.

Tenderly she plucked off the last petal. "Maybe he does!" she said breathlessly as the petal fluttered to the ground. She was staring into space, starry-eyed, when Furry-Ball noticed a dark figure move from the other side of the meadow. It was Waddler, and as he approached, Posie did not see him. Furry-Ball tried as hard as he could to become invisible, but he need not have worried that he'd be seen. Waddler seemed to be blind to everything and everyone but Posie.

"Yes! He does!" said Waddler, breaking into her reverie.

Startled, Posie looked up. For the second time in her life, she blushed. Waddler seemed amused at her surprise. He stepped forward and then, looking at her tenderly, said, "Well, I *do* love you."

"And I love you, Waddler," answered Posie shyly.

This was too much for Furry! This love stuff was getting too close for comfort. Who could guess what else might happen? Furry-Ball had to do something to protect himself, so once again he covered his eyes, and that small gesture was responsible for what happened next. Furry-Ball lost his balance, and that caused a little rock underneath his foot to roll. That, in turn, started another rock rolling, and in seconds, Furry-Ball was part of a giant rock slide. He was gaining such momentum that before he knew it, he landed in a heap right behind Posie.

"Furry!" was all that she could say as she whirled around in alarm. Once again, she blushed in embarrassment.

Without a word, Furry-Ball picked himself up. He was embarrassed, too, but more than that, he was thoroughly disgusted

with Posie and Waddler. *How can they get involved in all this love stuff?* he wondered. And yet, part of him was still very intrigued with it all. Both of these feelings mixed together until he felt totally confused. An awkward silence followed, and then the three raccoons smiled at each other. Smiles of embarrassment, to be sure. And then the smiles turned into laughs, and the laughs turned into great howls. Finally, weak from laughter, they returned to the others who were by now gathering decorations for the wedding. Furry-Ball could not forget what he had seen, but on the other hand, he could not bring himself to talk about it either. And so it was that he kept what he saw to himself.

It was later the next evening, and the wedding was over. It had been a beautiful ceremony. Seeker had read from The Book, and Honor and Giver had exchanged their straw rings and said their vows to each other. Then they had left for their wedding trip, and the guests had gone home. Aunt Serenity and Tidy-Paw were sweeping up the crumbs from the reception while Posie and Faith were taking down the flower garlands.

"I'm so glad that Needlenose came," Posie confided to Faith. "Maybe he'll follow The Maker, now that he's heard about Him from The Book."

Faith stopped her work for a moment. "I don't know what he thought about The Book or The Maker, but he certainly enjoyed the reception! I wonder what made him come!"

"I don't know, but he *did* eat quite a lot of the refreshments," added Posie.

Furry and Sunshine exchanged knowing glances. Furry-Ball smiled smugly. Their secret plan had worked. He smiled again. This was not the only secret he had! He thought of Posie and Waddler and what he had seen. *Perhaps The Maker, too, is smiling!* he thought.

$\mathcal{I}$ntegrity

The integrity of the Upright will guide them.
Proverbs 11:3

THE CLEARING beneath the log house fairly hummed with activity now that warmer weather had arrived. Seeker worked preparing daily readings from The Book and sermons to be given at the Gatherings. Tidy-Paw and Aunt Serenity prepared nourishing meals for the family, Waddler and Trasher had almost finished translating some of the more important parts of The Book for the foreigners, and Posie and Faith continued their work at the clinic. Farther away, Rapid and the newlyweds, Honor and Giver, had begun a new Gathering deep in the heart of enemy territory. Even Puddly and Truster were busy, according to the messages they had sent home. Their work was progressing, though they hadn't been heard from recently.

But, by far, the busiest of them all were Furry-Ball and Sunshine. Though they were always careful to obey their elders, they attached a new importance to obeying The Maker. So, they got up early to do their family chores and then used the rest of the day to accomplish secret projects for The Maker. It was as if they worked directly for Him, and they took their work very seriously. Nor did they feel a need to tell anyone about their projects. It was enough just to sense The Maker's smile on their work.

Sometimes they left messages and food for the bandits with the promise that there would be more at the next Gathering. It was not at all surprising, then, that attendance increased, and the family was amazed as more and more bandits came.

Needlenose was becoming a regular attender, and the family could not get over the change in his behavior. If they had not been so pleased with his presence, they might have been amused at his clumsy attempts to use manners as he slurped his food.

Often, while reaching for seconds, he made remarks like, "Right nice of you to invite me to this feed, er, I mean, Gathering." And once as he stuffed some of Sarah's candy into his mouth, he commented, "Mighty tasty bomb-bombs!"

But that was not all they did for their enemies. One day, as Furry-Ball and Sunshine walked through the forest, they noticed Upright markings scratched on a tree. Though neither one could remember whose idea it was, they began to scratch their own slogans, straight from their hearts, on tree stumps, rotten logs, and rocks. At first they wrote warnings like, "Follow The Maker *OR ELSE!*" Then they crossed out *"OR ELSE!"* and wrote *"PLEASE."* Gradually, they chose more gentle reminders translated from The Book like, "Believe on The Maker and you will be saved." But all were read and reread by their enemies.

And then they also continued to place leaves from The Book in the traps set by the Upright. Almost every day they were taken, and so they replaced them with new ones. One day, they actually came upon the Upright sitting by the brook, intently reading one of the leaves. They noticed, with relief, that no new traps had been set. However, the old ones still remained.

"Good," said Sunshine. "It takes him so long to read the leaves that he doesn't have time to set new traps!"

But perhaps the biggest change came in the hearts of the two youngest raccoons. Ever since they had first realized that there were plenty of opportunities to serve The Maker right in their own backyard, they did not seem to have enough hours in the day. And though they yearned for the time when they could be foreign missionaries like their brothers, they were happy and content to be at home serving The Maker.

One day when Furry-Ball and Sunshine were scouting for food in the silver treasure chest behind the Big House, the sound of Upright voices alerted them to danger. They ran for cover, and then, their curiosity getting the better of them, they peered out between the branches. "It's their weekly Gathering, all right," Sunshine concluded.

"It's strange that Sarah isn't there, though." Furry-Ball looked concerned.

They watched together as the last Upright went in, and the strange, but now familiar, sounds began. Listening for a moment, they were just about to turn away when two smaller Uprights approached the steps. One was undoubtedly Sarah. The two raccoons leaned forward, hoping to get a better glimpse of the other Upright.

"Tweeeeeet!" A shrill whistle coming from Furry-Ball pierced the silence and nearly sent Sunshine tumbling out into the open.

"Shhhhhh!" ordered Sunshine, who had never heard Furry-Ball make a sound like that. "What are you doing, Furry?" Then he regained his composure. "They'll hear us," he warned in a more gentle tone.

"I just did that to alert you," Furry-Ball explained. "They're gone now. We can talk," he whispered excitedly. "Did you see who it was? I'm sure it was the Upright boy! It looked just like him." He whistled again to emphasize his point.

"It couldn't have been," said Sunshine unconvinced. "He never goes in."

"But I saw him clearly. It had to be him! I'm certain!" Furry-Ball was adamant.

The unconvinced and the convinced sat there silently for a moment, neither of them budging from his position.

Then, not getting anywhere in the argument, Sunshine changed the subject. "How did you make that sound, Furry? It sounded just like Grandfather's whistle!"

"Tweeeeeet!" responded Furry-Ball. "I don't know," he said with a shrug, pursing his lips and whistling again.

"Did you learn it from Grandfather?"

"Well, yes. Once Grandfather did give me a lesson. But it's real easy. You do it," he said encouragingly.

Sunshine tried. All the way home he tried. But try as he might, he could not whistle.

It was later that afternoon, and the family members were preparing for their evening meal when Waddler and Posie burst into the clearing. They had been out for a walk together, but now they were breathless with excitement.

"We saw him!" they exclaimed. "The Upright boy! And he was in the Big House!"

Posie caught her breath and repeated the news. "We were passing the Big House, and we saw him coming out. He was with Sarah!" She paused to catch her breath again.

"Who?" questioned Seeker anxiously.

"The one who wore my tail on his hat," Waddler said quietly.

They stared at Waddler in disbelief. All except for Furry-Ball and Sunshine, who exchanged knowing glances. And then Furry-Ball broke the silence with a whistle, and for a second time everyone stared in disbelief.

It was like the shock of coming around a corner and meeting someone from out of the past, face to face. The whistle brought back so many memories that they almost expected to see Methuselah himself walk into their midst. But their joy lasted for only a moment, and then they realized the truth—it was Furry-Ball who had whistled, not Methuselah.

They talked about it that night over a delicious meal of nuts and dried berries—how much they still missed Methuselah, and yet how much their lives revolved around the principles he had taught them. They rejoiced in their memories of him, and now they rejoiced still more that the enemy Upright had gone into the Big House. No one except Furry-Ball and Sunshine had any idea of how it was that he went in, and they kept their project a secret.

And as for Furry-Ball's whistle, they could not flatter him enough on his newfound talent. It reminded them so much of their beloved Methuselah. It was not surprising that they spent the rest of the evening recalling all of his ways and the words with which he had guided them. In fact, they felt as if Methuselah were still very much with them.

$\mathcal{F}$orgotten

The Upright shall dwell in thy presence.
Psalm 140:13

ELP!" WAS all that it said. The tattered letter Furry-Ball clutched was barely legible, but it was Truster's handwriting, they were sure.

Whether they needed to go and help was not the question. Rather, it was *who* would go? Seeker called them all together and settled the matter quickly. No one dared disagree.

"Waddler, you and Trasher must go, and Furry-Ball and Sunshine will be your assistants," he announced. The two younger boys beamed with pride.

But their hearts were heavy as they packed the Upright-mover with supplies. Somberly, they said their farewells and prayed for The Maker's help. And then the four of them were gone. But long after they had gone, questions hung in the air like a thick fog. What had happened, and where was Puddly?

Perhaps it was a good thing that they didn't know what had happened and couldn't see Puddly, because at that very moment, Puddly was lying under a thick bough. He was weak and sick. He was thirsty and tired. He was lonely and discouraged. In fact, never before in his whole life had he ever been so miserable. And he had good reason to feel all of these things. He had sent Truster for help, but help had not come, and now he was sure that he was dying.

It would be impossible to know what Puddly was thinking about had he not begun to talk aloud. In a very weak voice, this is what he said: "Wasn't it enough, Dear Maker?" (He couldn't bring himself to speak to The Maker in any other way.) "Wasn't it enough? I didn't have to come here. I was only trying to please You. You know how hard we worked to learn their language. Oh, I know it wasn't Your fault that they hated us. But we kept on trying even when they ganged up on us and chased us away. Have You forgotten, Dear Maker, how mean they were to us? If You have, a look at my scars should remind You. It was hard not to fight back, but remember, we didn't even say bad things to them. We took it. And it was for *You* we did it." Puddly sighed.

"And then came the sickness. Truster and I never saw such disgusting things, but we went in and tried to help them. And for what? They chased us away even when we brought them water. Still we kept on. And only when Truster and I caught the sickness did we stop. And now, Dear Maker, just when Truster is well and able to go for help, now when I need Your help most of all, You leave me alone. He should have been back by now. It's been too long. I'm alone and too sick to go for water. Only You can help, but where are You? Have You forgotten me?"

A loud peal of thunder echoed through the forest, putting an end to Puddly's rantings. Gathering what strength he had left, he rolled over to look up at the sky. It was dark, oh, so very dark, and soon the whole forest was filled with the sound of falling raindrops. That is, everywhere except under the bough where Puddly lay. His thoughts turned more bitter than ever, and once again he spoke aloud.

"So You have enough rain for the whole forest except for here. You couldn't spare even a drop for me." And then suddenly, Puddly felt very ashamed. It was true. He was very disappointed in The Maker, but for the first time, he felt more disappointed in himself. He closed his eyes. "Forgive me, Dear Maker," he prayed. "I have no right to accuse You. You are The Maker, and You do what's best. Even if it means that I might die." Puddly waited for death to come, but nothing happened.

And then something did happen, though it didn't seem very remarkable at first. High in the branches overhead, a single raindrop joined several others and rolled down a slender branch toward the tip. There, they joined another group of drops, and these fell to some needles below, already laden with moisture. This, in turn, tipped the scale, causing the entire branch to bend, and in doing so, myriad raindrops splashed onto the lower branches. And though the boughs were very thick, one single drop fell through a tiny opening right above Puddly's head, and it landed right on his parched tongue.

It was only a drop, but it might as well have been a waterfall. Puddly opened his eyes. Was he imagining it? Another drop fell. Then another and another. Puddly wept for joy. And all through the night, the drops continued to fall into his open mouth. Then at last he slept peacefully.

When he awoke, his lips were wet with rain. He licked them and realized that for the first time his mouth was no longer dry. He felt cool and refreshed and even stronger. Reaching for a

rain-soaked branch overhead, he shook it until his fur was wet and then lapped up what he could.

He noticed the faint beginnings of dawn, and then at last golden streams of light penetrated the darkness of the thick branches, as if reaching into Puddly's very soul. He felt hope, and once again, he spoke aloud to The Maker.

"Why is it, Dear Maker, that I thought You had forgotten me?" He sighed in embarrassment. "I see now that it was I who had forgotten You." He sighed again. "And how could I have forgotten? It was You who guided us safely here and You who protected us from danger. And You who made Truster well . . . and now," he reminded himself, "You who have brought the rain when I needed it most. Oh, thank You, Dear Maker, thank You. Help me never to forget You again—even when things don't go well." His stomach rumbled, but he didn't care. He knew The Maker hadn't forgotten him.

And then, for the second time, something remarkable happened. A lone figure approached the bough that covered Puddly. He came stealthily, looking from side to side as if he were afraid someone were watching him. He was ragged in appearance, and mud clung to his fur. His ears were notched, proof that he had been in many fights. Great clumps of fur were missing, and even his paws were covered with scars.

He came quietly, but Puddly heard him and held his breath. A branch moved slightly, then another. Puddly had only time to whisper a word to The Maker. *"Help!"*

And then the branches parted and that awful face peered through. It was his enemy—he recognized him immediately. Puddly braced himself for the attack, but none came. Instead, his enemy was smiling. Could it be? Puddly squinted as he tried to make some sense out of it. And then the enemy reached out with some food in his paw and spoke. Now Puddly's language study had not progressed to the point where he could understand every word, but he did understand four words: "For you, sick, food."

Grateful to his enemy and to The Maker, Puddly bowed his head and whispered, "Thank You, Dear Maker." Then he ate hungrily.

And that is how they found him later when Truster led the four to Puddly. He was well, and seated around him were his former enemies, listening intently to Puddly as he told them about The Maker in their own language.

etour

*Righteousness keepeth him that is
Upright in the way.*
Proverbs 13:6

I T WAS the worst day of her life, and yet the best day.
Posie had waited. She had tried hard, oh, so hard, to be
patient, and yet no word came from the absent missionaries.
The rest of the family gathered daily for prayer after reading from
The Book, and yet nothing changed as each day went by. And
the worst of it was that no one seemed to be alarmed.

"Be patient, Little Flower," was all that Seeker said when she
came to him with her fears.

"The Maker'll answer our prayers in His own good time,
Dear," Aunt Serenity said when she went to her for encouragement.

"Keep busy serving The Maker, and the time will go more
quickly, Dear," assured Tidy-Paw when Posie seemed anxious.

How Posie wished for a word—any word—from the missionaries! Even Faith's words of encouragement didn't seem to
cheer her. And so it was that, more and more, Posie went for
long walks by herself. No one seemed to understand how she
felt—at least that is what she thought. And as she spent more
time worrying over the missionaries (especially Waddler), she
spent less time trusting The Maker for their safety.

On this particular day, the sun was up, and apart from her
gloomy feelings, Posie thought that the forest had never looked
so beautiful. The tall firs were washed with fresh dew, and the

birds sang so sweetly that for a while she felt lost in the beauty of her surroundings. Coming to an open meadow, she caught the fragrant scent of purple lupine. She picked a bouquet and then went about the happy task of weaving her wreath.

It was good to be away from all her dreary thoughts, and it was also good to be away from the rest of the family with their well-meant, but unhelpful advice. It wasn't that she didn't love them—it was just that she thought of herself as an adult now and didn't need their advice. They just didn't understand how she felt. Grandfather would have understood, she knew, but he was gone now, and so it was better to be by herself. She continued to weave her wreath, pushing all her dreary thoughts away as she worked.

A rustle in a bush nearby caught her attention. Looking up, she froze momentarily as an unfamiliar raccoon stepped out. He was young and tall, and he smiled disarmingly.

"My name's Warrior," he stated matter-of-factly. He walked slowly toward her in a friendly and nonthreatening manner, stopping a short distance away.

She relaxed slightly and then turned to her weaving again, still feeling a bit awkward and uncomfortable.

"Are you waiting for someone?" he asked politely.

"No . . . no one in particular," she answered, still weaving her wreath. She didn't know why she felt so uncomfortable.

"Do you come here every day?" he continued to press her.

"Sometimes I do," she answered hesitantly.

"That's a mighty pretty wreath. In fact, the only thing prettier is the girl who's weaving it," he complimented her.

Posie blushed, and her uneasiness began to fade. After all, he was saying such nice things. She was just about to thank him for the compliment when he spoke again.

"I have to go now, but I'll come back tomorrow. Will you be here?" he asked hopefully.

"I'm not sure," Posie answered, her doubts returning.

And then he was gone, and Posie was left to her thoughts. *I wonder who he is. He seemed so polite, and he thinks I'm pretty.* She felt almost disappointed that he had gone. She sat there for a long time, and the more she thought about this stranger and what he had said, the more she forgot about the missionaries and thought only about herself. It had been a long time, she admitted, since she had looked at herself in the reflecting pool. Could it be true? Was she, in fact, pretty? It was such a beautiful day, and the brook was not far. Surely, she had enough time to take a detour on her way home, and besides, she simply had to know if what this stranger had said was true.

She started out for the brook, and as she did so, the birds sang more sweetly than ever, making her feel that her intentions were totally innocent. Even the breeze, bringing the delicious scent of sun-dried fir needles, encouraged her onward.

How could one little look be wrong? she reasoned. So caught up in her thoughts was she that she forgot all about the missionaries, her family—even The Maker Himself. All she really wanted to do was to look into the reflecting pool.

Out of breath, she could hardly wait as she heard the water gurgling and splashing ahead. And then, there it was—the brook, and off to the side, the mirror-like water of the reflecting pool. She hurried over and looked down.

For a moment, she stood there speechless. *It's true!* she exclaimed. *I am rather pretty!* She tilted her wreath at a different angle, and then moved her head from side to side, thoroughly enjoying what she saw. *The stranger was right,* she admitted to herself. (Now, sometimes one wrong action can lead to another and another; and this is exactly what happened to Posie.) She began to weigh the possibility of meeting the stranger again. Perhaps he would say more nice things to her. She was so lost in her own reflection that she did not hear the quiet footsteps of Faith as she approached the brook to look for messages from the missionaries.

A twig snapped as Faith stepped out of the forest and saw in one glance what Posie was doing. Posie whirled around and faced her. Neither said a word, but in that moment it seemed to each of them that a hundred years went by. As Posie stared into Faith's eyes, she tried to read her expression. What was it she saw? Was it shock or disappointment or hurt? No, it was the combination

of all of these feelings into one—betrayal. And yet, in spite of what Posie saw, there was also a sense of tender caring that shone through. In contrast, Posie's own head hung down, and her face reflected shame and guilt because in the deepest part of her heart, Posie knew that she had betrayed her best friend as well as The Maker Himself.

Then, just as suddenly as she had come, Faith turned with a sob and hurried away, leaving Posie to her thoughts. She stood there helplessly for a long time, wishing with all her heart that she had never come there. She felt so ashamed and disgusted with herself. But most of all, a feeling of anger crept over her—an anger so great that she could not even cry. *What's wrong with me?* she asked herself accusingly. *Where did it all start?* she continued, demanding an answer of herself. But before she could even think of an answer, a far-off clap of thunder interrupted her thoughts. Looking toward the west, she noticed dark, threatening clouds approaching and, with them, the first drops of rain.

Her thoughts turned to safety, and she dove under a bush for cover. Almost immediately, a bolt of lightning lit up the sky. And

though the winds blew and the rain fell rapidly around her, she found herself more involved with the storm of betrayal in her own life—she had betrayed herself and Faith and Waddler and, most of all, The Maker.

"Oh, why did I have to go to the reflecting pool?" she moaned. "It was because I believed the stranger's compliments," she answered herself truthfully. "But why did I listen to him in the first place?" She struggled to admit the real reason, and then, slowly, very slowly, the words came out. "It was because I forgot The Maker." She saw it so plainly—how she had not wanted to take her family's advice to wait patiently for The Maker's answer, how she had let herself feel that no one understood her worries and so had gone for more and more walks by herself, and then how her loneliness had made her open to the stranger's flattering words.

She realized all this in a moment, and it was then that she cried. Never before had she felt such shame. She had betrayed her Maker and Faith and Waddler, and she felt that things would never be the same again. Never again could she be called The Maker's follower—she did not feel worthy. Never again would Faith believe in her. And never again could she face Waddler. Her body heaved in great sobs. No longer did she believe in herself or even like herself, nor did she care that the storm came closer and closer.

She cried for such a long time that no more tears would come, and her mouth felt dry, though not nearly as dry as her heart felt. At last, gasping for air, she turned her face upward, hoping for even a breath of the wind that was howling outside her shelter. The air around her was stifling, and to make it worse, it was so dark that she could hardly see at all.

She lay there in this state, feeling numb and lifeless. Nothing mattered to her anymore, not even being alive. But suddenly, a mosquito bit her right on the end of her nose, reminding her that she was still very much alive. She swatted the annoying insect away with her paw and gloomily went back to her dark thoughts. *If only The Maker would let a tree fall on my shelter,* she thought, *then at last my life would be ended.* But nothing happened. Instead, the storm continued to rage around her.

And yet, something *was* happening. The longer she lay there, the more she wished with all her heart that she had not betrayed The Maker. And the more she wished this, the more she hoped that The Maker could forgive her. She could not remember what The Book said about this problem, but she decided to take the chance and approach The Maker. So, summoning all her courage, she spoke aloud.

"Dear Maker, it's me—Your unfaithful follower. How I wish I hadn't taken this detour to the reflecting pool!" Then with the eyes of her heart she saw things even more plainly. "It really was a detour from *You* that I took." She sighed, and then in a very small voice she said pleadingly, "But would You, I mean could You, forgive me, Dear Maker? I *do* want to follow You again. I know Faith will never believe in me again, and I can never face Waddler either. But, Dear Maker, I can't live without You, so if You won't forgive me . . ." Her voice trembled as she spoke, "I guess I might as well die."

There. It was out at last. She had said those words, and now she awaited The Maker's response. She did not wait long. A blinding flash of lightning streaked across the sky. She braced herself for the thunder, but was not prepared for the loud crack that followed—and then the sickening noise of the falling tree, coming from right above her.

TTHHUUDD! It hit, shaking the very ground on which Posie lay. And she knew what it felt like to be dead. She lay there

for a long time, feeling quite dead until another mosquito bit her—this time on her ear.

Wait a minute! she addressed what she thought to be her dead self. *If I'm dead, how come I felt a mosquito?* Gathering all her courage, she tried to lift her paw. To her amazement, she found that it still worked. She sat up and carefully parted some branches to look out. There, only inches away, lay the trunk of a giant fir tree. Posie's whole body shook from fear—she had narrowly missed death! Suddenly, she was glad to be alive. Courage flooded into her whole being like a wave, and she was just about to address The Maker when, again, a peal of thunder echoed across the sky. She covered her ears with her paws, filled with the dread that this time her life would not be spared. Again, the sickening crack and sound of a falling tree. TTHHUUDD! Again, the shaking of the ground, but this time Posie's body continued to shake. Only then did she realize that she was still very much alive.

"I'm alive, alive!" she shouted in great relief. Yet it was very dark in her shelter, and she had no visible proof of this fact. She pinched herself. It was true—she *was* alive! How wonderful that pain felt! *Oh, it's so good to be alive!* she exclaimed to herself in utter joy. Never had she so appreciated being alive before, and yet total darkness surrounded her. But though she sat there unable to see a thing, she knew in her heart that for the first time in her life she saw things clearly.

She saw that her life, even though filled with problems and mistakes, was very precious to her after all. She had the feeling that perhaps others still saw her life as precious too. And as the sounds of the storm disappeared, a faint hope stirred deep inside her heart—a hope that welled up and came out at last, though only in a whisper. "Oh, Dear Maker, have You given my life back because You see it as precious too? Could it be that You *do* forgive me?" And though nothing had improved in her outward condition, she sat there quietly in total peace, knowing that The Maker did indeed forgive her, and that she could trust Him to help her.

The sun shone through the clouds at last, but Posie saw nothing of this in her darkened shelter. Nor could she find her way out of that tangled evergreen maze. She sat very still and listened intently. At last came a faint noise—the familiar sound of someone calling her. It was Faith. Help had finally come.

"I'm here! I'm here!" she shouted as loudly as she could.

The others soon arrived, and together, they lifted the heavy branches, at last allowing Posie to climb to freedom. Then they stood there surveying the two fallen giants.

Seeker spoke. "The Maker be praised! The first tree missed your shelter by a few inches. But look at what happened to the second." He gestured toward a huge trunk lying diagonally on top of the first. "If the first had not fallen on that spot, the second would have fallen directly on Posie's shelter, and she . . . would be . . ." He wiped a tear from his eye. "Oh, Little Flower, to think that we almost lost you!" He hugged her tightly.

Soon the others were joining in, and Posie thought that she would explode with gratefulness for just being alive and belonging to such a wonderful family. She knew that she had words of apology to say to Faith, but they could wait.

And that is how it was that this day, though it had started out as her worst, had become her best.

CHAPTER 25

The Return

No good thing will He withhold from those
who walk Uprightly.
Psalm 84:11

NOTHING HAD changed, yet everything seemed different to Posie. Her life had become very precious to her since she had nearly lost it, and yet she did not try to hang on to it in a miserly fashion either. In fact, the opposite was true. She was there to help at every opportunity, and she took very little time for herself except to eat and sleep. And even in sleep, she found herself dreaming of new challenges.

She was sitting with Faith on a rock upstream from the message center one day discussing one of these new challenges.

"If only we could do something for all the homeless," she said to Faith wistfully. "Ever since the storm, there are so many more than usual."

"It's true," agreed Faith, "and having to find new homes has meant less time to hunt for food. They seem so thin, and several are sick."

"That's it!" exclaimed Posie. "Food! That's what we can do! We can gather more food. If we started a food center, we'd always be ready for any emergency." She started to get up, but as she did so, her foot slipped, plunging her into the edge of the water. She grabbed onto a stick to steady herself and was about to step out of the water when she noticed a piece of bark caught in a crevice of the rock by her foot.

Faith saw it at the same time and, reaching for it, fell into the water alongside Posie. "A message!" she managed to sputter.

Together they laughed at their common misfortune, and then excitedly climbed up on the rock to read what they found. It *was* a message—the first they had received since Waddler and the others had left to help Puddly and Truster. "All is well. Will return soon," the message read.

"I'm so glad!" Posie hugged Faith in relief. "Let's tell the others!" They jumped off the rock and hurried home, not even taking time to shake the water from their fur.

It was a joyful family that heard the news that day. "We can always count on The Maker!" exclaimed Seeker. "The Maker heard our prayers!" added Tidy-Paw. Aunt Serenity just smiled an "I told you so" smile.

But once the news was shared, Posie could not spare a minute more in idle chatter. She politely excused herself to start on her new project—gathering food for the homeless. Faith joined her, and by evening, they had stored enough to distribute the next day.

Early the next morning, they set out, carrying as much food as they could. It was barely light, and as they walked, Posie nearly tripped over her first homeless raccoon. He was sleeping out in the open, and by his thin frame, she could tell that he had not eaten in a while.

"Shhh!" whispered Posie. "Let's not wake him—let's just leave him some food."

Without bothering to wake him, they put a neat bundle next to him with a note: "From The Maker." Then they hurried on. Before long, Faith saw another of the homeless. She, too, was sleeping, and next to her were three small babies. They repeated their errand of mercy, leaving them the last of the food and with it a note: "From The Maker."

Just before they arrived at the brook, Posie saw a familiar figure lying asleep just off the path. It was Warrior, she was sure. "I can't take the chance that he'll wake up, Faith. I don't want to talk to him, but he needs our help. Would you go back for more food?" she whispered. "I'll go on to the brook and wait for you there, and I promise that I won't go near the reflecting pool." Her face showed her determination.

Faith left to get the food, and Posie hurried to the message center, carefully avoiding the reflecting pool. She sat down in the sun, a little tired from all her work, but happy to be in The Maker's service. The sun felt warm on her body, and she felt that warmth even in her heart.

"Oh, Dear Maker, somehow my life seems more precious than ever, and it's all because of You! Though I'm glad that Waddler and the others are returning, I'm more glad that I have You. If I had no one else but You, Dear Maker, it would be enough!" Posie spoke these words aloud, but she looked to heaven as she spoke. Then she sighed in contentment. It was good to be The Maker's faithful follower.

The sound of the rushing water brought her back to reality. She looked over at the edge of the brook. A piece of bark, floating in the water, caught her eye. It was moving toward her, and in fact, it bumped right into the rock upon which she was sitting. It was a message, and she quickly bent down to get it.

"It's . . . for me! And it's . . . from Waddler!" she said breathlessly. Posie sat there frozen, almost afraid to read the letter. She was in this position when Faith arrived.

"Well, what does the message say?" asked Faith, anxious to hear the latest news.

"It's for me!" repeated Posie. "And it's from Waddler!"

"Well, what does he say? Aren't you going to read it?" Faith's curiosity was getting the best of her.

Posie was just about to read the message when she saw something else attached to it—something all wrapped in leaves. Her agile fingers strained to break a vine tying this object to the letter, but then her eyes caught the words on the letter and her heart almost stopped. Slowly, ever so slowly, she read the words aloud.

"Dear . . . Posie, . . . Will . . . you . . . marry . . . me? . . . Love . . . Waddler." Her mouth fell open, but she could not speak.

Faith's giggle broke the silence. "Aren't you going to open the package?" She knew that Posie's curiosity would motivate her into action.

With fingers flying, Posie tore away the leaf covering until the very last leaf was gone. And then, there it was! The tiny object was exposed. Together, they stared in disbelief at what they saw—a delicate silver circle wound around the most beautiful stone they had ever seen. It sparkled and shone, and both girls knew what it was immediately.

"A silver band!" exclaimed Posie. "He must have made it himself. And it means that he loves me and wants to marry me."

"Well?" asked Faith, her face beaming.

Posie didn't answer in words. She just put the ring (for of course that's what the silver band was) on her finger, and her radiant smile said it all.

Faith smiled, too, and hugged her warmly. "This means a wedding!" she said excitedly.

Posie nodded, her face aglow. The two talked for a long time. But then Posie got very serious, as if something very important had crossed her mind. "Faith, I want to always remember that I am, first of all, The Maker's, and second, Waddler's. That means that we don't have a minute to lose. There are more homeless to help, and right now that is my first concern."

"You're right," said Faith, a bit dejected. "But I do hope we can take time to plan the wedding. It must be as beautiful as the Uprights'—and you *do* remember how beautiful theirs was!" She sighed wistfully.

"We'll have time, Faith. But, come, we can't waste any more time now," she reminded her, and so arm in arm, they started back to their work in the forest.

It wasn't long before they came upon the mother and babies they had helped a short while before. Haggard and gaunt, the mother trudged down the path ahead, with the three little ones barely able to keep up.

"Is there anything we can do to help?" asked Faith when she caught up to them.

"If only I could find a home," she said wearily. "I'm afraid the children won't make it much longer."

"I'll watch them until you return," offered Faith as she gathered them in her arms. "You go by yourself, and may The Maker help you find a home."

The mother was clearly overwhelmed with Faith's kindness. All she could say was "thank you," and then she turned and was gone. In what seemed like minutes, the children were sleeping, exhausted from their long walk.

"Why don't you look for others to help, Posie?" suggested Faith. "It'll take her some time to find a home big enough for this family. When you're finished, meet me here."

Posie took her advice and started out alone. To her, every life was precious, and she was anxious to find any and all who needed their help. Her black eyes peered beneath thick branches, while her ears strained for any sound that told of the presence of a stranger. However, neither of these senses alerted her. Rather, it was a certain smell—the smell of sickness—that caught her attention. She followed this smell until she felt that she would become sick, and then, under a bush and nearly covered with leaves, she saw him.

It was Rubbish. He was covered with mud, and blood was matted in his fur. His eyes were shut, but he was still breathing. Nearby lay a fallen tree that told the whole story. Posie bent down and took his paw in hers. She could not help the tear that trickled down her cheek. "Rubbish, I'm here to help," she whispered.

One eye fluttered, but quickly closed again. "Water," was all he said.

One part of her dreaded leaving him alone, and yet another urged her to act to save his life. Gently, very gently, she let go of his paw and slipped away to the brook for water.

At first, Rubbish did not respond, but gradually, as Posie gave him more water, he opened his eyes ever so slightly. At last his breathing became normal, and Posie knew he would live. She concentrated then on washing his matted fur, while at the same

time, cooling his fevered body. After a short while, he fell into a deep, relaxed sleep.

Posie, not realizing that she was at the point of exhaustion, reached over one more time to pour water on his wounds. Instead, she spilled the water, and her outstretched paw slipped to the ground below. She was asleep.

And that was how Waddler found her. He had returned with the other missionaries, and while the others had a joyful reunion in the clearing, Waddler set out to look for Posie and Faith. It was his sense of smell, too, that led him to the spot where Rubbish lay. And there, next to him, lay Posie, her paw still stretched out, holding an empty shell.

Waddler stood there for a moment, greatly relieved to find her at last. And as he looked at her, he realized what had happened. Suddenly, he was overcome with emotion. He saw the ring on her finger, and it told him that she had promised herself to him. But he also saw her outstretched paw. She had fallen asleep out of sheer exhaustion in the very act of service. Waddler could not

help himself. He wept. He wept for Posie's tiredness, but he also wept for joy that The Maker would give him a wife who thought of others before herself. For a long time, Waddler kept his vigil. He did not wish to wake her from her much needed sleep.

And when at last Posie did wake up, she could not believe her eyes.

"Waddler! At last you've returned!" was all that she could say.

But in the end, it was not all that she said. And Waddler had some things to say too!

CHAPTER 26

*W*edding Plans

The LORD knows the days of the Upright,
and their inheritance shall be forever.
Psalm 37:18

I T WAS official—Waddler and Posie were to be married! And there was no one more excited than Posie, though outwardly, there seemed to be no one more indifferent. For one thing, she was nowhere to be found. It wasn't that she was purposely hiding. On the contrary, she was busy from early morning until almost dark working in the clinic or taking food to the homeless.

And why this seeming indifference to her own wedding? Posie dearly loved Waddler and had told him so. But she also knew that she loved The Maker more and never wanted it to be otherwise. She could not quite forgive herself for forgetting The Maker, and so to make sure that it would never happen again, she vowed that she would not give in to the temptation of putting her own plans above The Maker's work.

She continued to stay far away from the reflecting pool, knowing that The Maker's approval was more important than her self-approval. And as best she could, she tried to explain all this to Waddler and the others, who, though they didn't share her problem, tried very hard to understand. For this reason, they decided to take action and plan the wedding themselves.

Tidy-Paw and Aunt Serenity supervised the preparation of the food that had been gathered and transported on the Upright-mover, while Seeker spent hours preparing the wedding sermon.

Puddly and Trasher wrote the invitations and then saw to it that all their friends (and enemies) got them.

Faith did not seem to have any particular job, but desperately wished that she did. To be truthful, she was disappointed that the wedding plans seemed to lack the festive air that she had always dreamed about. Yet she dared not tempt Posie to get involved in festivities when she seemed to be trying so hard to put The Maker first. And so, to go along with Posie's wishes, she faithfully helped with the food and tried to forget her dreams. No one was more surprised than she, therefore, when one day Posie ran breathlessly into the clearing with some exciting news.

"Oh, if only you could have seen it!" she blurted out.

"What?" demanded Faith.

"The Upright wedding! It was just as Furry-Ball told us!" She panted as she tried to catch her breath.

"But how did you see it?" asked Faith, knowing that Posie could never have reached the clear stone opening by herself.

"It was outside!" exclaimed Posie, "Next to the Big House." Her breathing returned to normal again. "Oh, if only you had been there, Faith!"

Now at this point, Faith perked up. For the first time in many days, Posie's interest in weddings had come alive. It reminded her of days in the past when they loved to discuss weddings— particularly Upright weddings. Careful not to tempt her, yet curious about what Posie had seen, Faith answered. "Well, I wasn't there, so why don't you tell me what you saw?"

Posie's eyes took on a faraway look and then she started. "Well, I was on my way home from the clinic when I heard beautiful sounds, and they reminded me of Grandfather's whistle.

The sounds were coming from near the Big House, so I climbed up the wall, and the first thing I saw was a beautiful cake with pink flowers on a table quite close by, and then . . . there they were!" Posie's words came tumbling out more quickly than Faith could understand. She stopped herself and then started again.

"The Uprights, I mean—they were all there having a wedding outside the Big House. Even Sarah! She wore a flower wreath and sprinkled pink petals all down the path. And a little Upright carried a golden band on something soft that looked like moss. And then they came—the woman Upright and the man! And they stood under a beautiful rainbow of flowers!" Posie's eyes became dreamy.

"Well, what did they wear?" asked Faith anxiously. She was glad that at last Posie was showing such excitement about weddings.

(Now, it is interesting to note that Posie did not see what you and I would have seen had we been there. She totally missed the bride's beautiful dress—perhaps because raccoons know that their fur is far more lovely than the loveliest dress. Instead, she saw something else.)

"She wore a wreath of the whitest Avalanche Lilies," she said almost reverently, "and falling from it was . . . a . . ."

"A what?" Faith pleaded with her to finish.

"A waterfall—but it didn't look wet!" Posie replied to her startled listener. "It was so beautiful," she continued. "Oh, if only . . . ," and then she stopped herself. "But we have so much work to do." Her thoughts returned to reality, and her paws instinctively reached to help with the food.

It was Faith's turn to look off into space dreamily. "A waterfall that isn't wet," she repeated slowly as she tried to picture it. And then, as if something had suddenly popped into her mind, Faith excused herself and quickly slipped away into the forest. She knew right where to go, and within minutes found it—a large and almost perfect spiderweb. "Yes!" she exclaimed. "A waterfall that isn't wet!"

Faith stood there in utter amazement at her discovery. "This would be perfect, and it wouldn't be tempting Posie if *I* do it for her," she said aloud. "I could find more spider webs and make a lovely waterfall. . . ." And then she laughed at the idea of a waterfall that wasn't wet.

She was still laughing when another thought suddenly occurred to her, and then she sighed wistfully. "Oh, but wet water-

falls are so lovely. If only . . ." She thought for a moment, and then her eyes widened as if she visualized something very clearly. "That's it!" she nearly shouted with joy. With that, she returned to the clearing, her mind brimming with new ideas on how to make Posie's wedding as beautiful as the weddings of the Uprights.

Early the next morning, Faith slipped out quietly and ran into the forest, scouting out every spider web she could find, and to her delight, every one of them was studded with sparkling beads of dew. "Thank You, Dear Maker, for the wet waterfalls!" she exclaimed aloud, feeling all the more certain that her idea was a good one. Then she returned quietly to the clearing for breakfast.

It was hard to wait, but no sooner had Posie and Waddler left to do their work than Faith gathered the rest and told them of her ideas.

"We need some very special flowers for her wreath," she said. "The Uprights had Avalanche Lilies, Posie told me. If only we could get some for her, they would be the perfect flowers!"

"But where can we find Avalanche Lilies?" asked Trasher, who knew only too well that they grew on the highest slopes of the mountains.

Faith's expression fell. "If only we could find some," she said, remembering how Posie had talked about their whiteness.

Puddly broke in. "We still have time," he reminded them. "It's worth a try." He looked over at Trasher hopefully.

"You're right, Puddly," he admitted. Then he smiled more agreeably. "After all, it will be her only wedding."

"And then the music," continued Faith. "Furry-Ball, could you teach Sunshine how to whistle so that you can play some wedding music together?" She did not wait for an answer from them, but added, "You can go to the Big House every day and listen to the sounds and practice them over and over again."

Now Furry-Ball would much rather have played a solo, but not wanting to dampen Faith's enthusiasm, he grudgingly agreed to try, though he did not hold out much hope for Sunshine's abilities.

"Truster," Faith now turned to a new subject, "how can we make a flower rainbow?" Her voice expressed some doubt about this project.

Truster thought a while and then came up with an idea. "I don't know about the flower part, but I could find a new branch to bend into a rainbow if you could weave flowers around it."

"That would work perfectly!" she said excitedly, visualizing it in her mind.

They all scurried off at last, leaving Faith alone with her thoughts. *How can I make a cake?* she asked herself. Nothing Aunt Serenity and Tidy-Paw had ever made tasted like the cake she

remembered that Furry-Ball had found in the silver treasure chest. *I can't make one!* she finally had to admit to herself. She sat down, feeling that the whole wedding would be ruined if she could not have a wedding cake like the Uprights had. And then the word *Upright* triggered a new thought—maybe Sarah would make one.

Her hope soon turned to despair, however, when she realized that they could not even invite Sarah. Their enemies would be terrified of an Upright at the wedding. And how could they ask her to make a cake and then not invite her? She tossed these thoughts back and forth in her mind, until, totally bewildered, she went to Aunt Serenity for advice.

"Politeness and truthfulness always please The Maker, Dear." Then, with those principles in mind, together they composed a letter to Sarah. This is what they wrote: "Dear Sarah, Please come to Posie and Waddler's wedding next week in the meadow by the fallen tree, but could you stay out of sight so that you don't scare our enemies? Also, can you please bring a wedding cake?"

Faith and Aunt Serenity read it over and hoped they had said things truthfully and politely, and then Faith left it on the stone wall.

The next day, the letter was gone, and to her delight, a reply was waiting there. It said:

"I will be there (out of sight) and I *will* make a cake. Love, Sarah."

Faith was overjoyed. Everything was going smoothly, according to her plans, and now only the last-minute arrangements had to be completed. If only Trasher and Puddly would return from their trip to the mountain, and if only they would find the precious white lilies that Posie loved so much.

It was two days before the wedding. Aunt Serenity and Faith were weaving fir tips around the rainbow branch that Truster had chosen. It formed an almost perfect arch, under which the couple would stand.

"We can add the flowers at the last minute if they find enough lilies," suggested Faith. "Do you think The Maker cares whether they find them?" she asked Aunt Serenity.

"Now don't you fret, dear. The Book tells us plainly that just as The Maker dresses the lilies of the field, He provides for all our needs too." She gave Faith a gentle pat.

Faith accompanied Truster to the meadow where he promised to put the rainbow in place. They studied the area for a long time, and then chose a spot near the end of the path—just before it disappeared into the forest. The meadow itself was not very big, but it was a lovely place, surrounded by lush ferns and tall

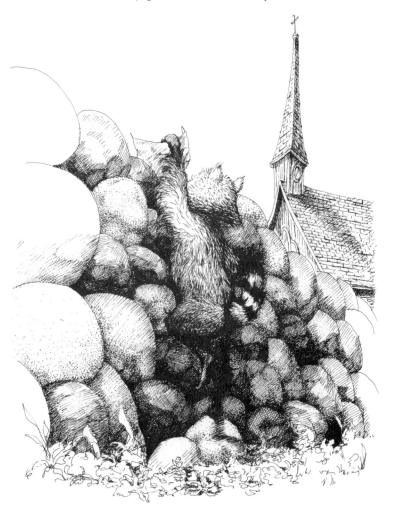

Douglas firs. Small clumps of wildflowers dotted the grass here and there, adding an air of festivity. Nearby was the Gathering House—too small to hold all the guests. Faith was glad that they had chosen to have the wedding outside. For this special ceremony, it seemed so appropriate somehow to be surrounded by all that was familiar and dear to them. Faith took one more look at Truster's handiwork, and then feeling totally satisfied, they returned home, hoping that Waddler and Posie would not pass that way.

It was now the day before the wedding, and Faith almost despaired when Trasher and Puddly did not return that morning. Everything else seemed to be on schedule. Furry-Ball and Sunshine were making great progress in their whistling, though Faith felt that they could have chosen slower and quieter songs. She decided to talk to them later and suggest that they slow the tempo a bit.

Meanwhile, she went about picking flowers for the bouquets, and she had just about resigned herself to a less than perfect wedding without the lilies when she heard the unmistakable sound of the Upright-mover coming through the forest. Looking up, she was unprepared for the sight that greeted her. There came Puddly and Trasher pulling a huge mountain of Avalanche Lilies on the mover.

"You found them!" she exclaimed, and tears welled up in her eyes. "And there's enough for her wreath and bouquet and even the rainbow! The Maker *does* care!"

And so it was that late that afternoon, when Posie came home from her work at the clinic, she found fresh white Avalanche Lilies laid carefully on the stone table with a note: "To our beloved sister for her wedding day. From Trasher and Puddly."

CHAPTER 27

The Wedding

The generation of the Upright will be blessed.
Psalm 112:2

I T WAS the day of days! Never had there been a day like it in the forest before, and for Posie and Waddler, never would there be a day like it again! It was a glorious day—crystal clear and just warm enough so that gentle breezes spread the delicate forest fragrances everywhere. The forest itself seemed to be celebrating on this special day.

Faith tiptoed past the others, still sleeping, and peeked out at the sky, just turning light. One look told her what she wanted to know. "It's going to be a beautiful wedding day!" she half whispered to herself in delight.

She had much to do on this special day. Gathering some of the Avalanche Lilies, she hurried off to the rainbow arch in the meadow and carefully tucked the lovely white flowers in among the fir tips. Standing back from her work, she had to admit that the effect was quite lovely. Then, using the rest of the lilies, she formed a beautiful bouquet for Posie, adding other flowers of the palest pink, and framing them all with ferns that cascaded down.

At last it was time for her most important work. Quickly and nervously, she gathered each of the spider webs that she had found, ever so careful not to shake the drops of dew that still clung to each strand. With deft paws, she skillfully crafted a veil, and when she was finished, it looked just as she had hoped—like a wet waterfall! She held it up to the sunlight, and the drops of dew shone and sparkled like diamonds. Satisfied with her efforts, she returned to finish her gift for Posie.

The others were up, and they were admiring Posie's wreath that she had left on the table.

"Her finest work," Tidy-Paw was saying.

"She never expected Avalanche Lilies!" said Seeker, looking at Puddly and Trasher with pride.

Faith placed the wedding veil on the table. No one spoke. They couldn't. It was exquisite—lacy and filmy and translucent and yet as natural and fresh as a waterfall! And with the little drops of dew still shimmering in the sunlight, it did indeed look like a wet waterfall!

Tidy-Paw and Aunt Serenity gently attached the fragile veil to Posie's flower wreath, and then stood back to watch as Posie returned from washing in the brook.

From the edge of the clearing, her eyes spotted the veil. She stared in amazement, then ran to the stone table, her gaze fixed

upon it. And yet she could not even so much as touch the magnificent piece.

"It's . . . it's . . . a waterfall . . . just like the Upright's!" she said in disbelief. "But it's much more beautiful!" Then, lifting her gaze, she looked at each one, her eyes brimming with tears. How could she ever thank them for this beautiful waterfall wedding veil? And how could she ever thank them for their love and care shown to her over and over again? They were her beloved family, and soon, she would be leaving them. She was not sure that she could. She did not even feel worthy of wearing the veil.

"It's too beautiful. I can't wear it!" she blurted out, and then she realized that her words did not really express how she felt. "I mean . . ."

The family looked at her tenderly, and Faith stepped forward. Gently, very gently, she lifted the veil and placed it carefully on Posie's head. And as everyone gazed in admiration, she stood there shyly, looking as beautiful as she ever had, and yet totally unaware of that beauty. Instead, at that moment, she saw only the beauty of her family, and she felt most unworthy of their love.

She tried again. "Thank you for this wonderful gift." She looked directly at Faith and Puddly and Trasher when she spoke. "But thank you more for loving me—each in your own special way. I don't feel that I am worthy of your love, but I am so thankful for each of you." She looked around her, and suddenly, her thoughts were filled with loving memories from her childhood, including those of Methuselah, though he was not in that circle now.

"I feel very rich," she said as she looked at them, "because all of you have given me gifts." They looked perplexed, so she explained further. "I mean gifts that are not wrapped—but gifts that will go with me for the rest of my life. Gifts of laughter," she looked at Furry-Ball and Sunshine; "and encouragement," she looked at Tidy-Paw and Seeker; "and wisdom," she looked at Aunt Serenity; "and strength," she looked at Trasher; "and commitment," she looked at Puddly; "and gentleness," she looked at Truster; "and understanding," she looked at Faith. "And today, I feel more thankful than ever for Grandfather's gift, too—belief in The Maker."

There was not a dry eye when they all gathered around her to ask The Maker's blessing on this special day.

Then, together, they started out for the wedding celebration. Posie rode on the Upright-mover with her lovely veil shimmering like a cascade of light, while the others pressed closely around her, knowing that soon she would be gone from them.

The sound of distant bells told them that the time for the celebration had come. Waddler, who was already at the Gathering House, was ringing them himself, and the sound echoed throughout the whole forest. As they arrived, they found many guests already there: Rapid with others he had brought; Giver and Honor with little Joy, who was to be the flower girl; and other friends from their Gathering. Needlenose, Rubbish, and many of the other bandits were there. Many of the patients from the clinic had come, along with the homeless who had been helped.

Posie looked over at the rainbow arch, dotted with white lilies. She thought the meadow had never looked so lovely. And then her eyes caught something else. Away from all the guests, guarded carefully by Furry-Ball and Sunshine, was a table laden with food, and in the middle was something that took Posie's breath away—a wedding cake sprinkled with pink flowers! She saw all of this in an instant, and her heart seemed to overflow within her. It was a miracle! *But where did it come from?* she wondered. Overwhelmed, she stood there for a long time trying to guess who had done this, when suddenly, she was aware of a strange, but familiar scent—the unmistakable Upright scent—of Sarah. It was slight, and though no one else seemed to notice, Posie knew that she was there. Could Sarah have made the cake? And if so, where was she?

Her heart pounded as her eyes searched everywhere, and had not the breeze brought the fresh scent from above, Posie might never have seen her. She looked up furtively. Peeking out from between two boughs was the familiar face she had come to love so dearly. And then the little hand waved, the signal of friendship between them. Posie looked around. No one was watching at the moment, and so, pretending to adjust her veil, she lifted her paw and waved very discreetly. A smile spread across Sarah's face, and Posie thought her own heart would burst with joy.

This all happened in a fleeting moment, and then Faith came to hand out the bouquets. Joy and Faith carried bouquets of the most delicate wildflowers in colors of pink, purple, yellow, and blue. But Posie thought hers was the most beautiful of all— snow-white Avalanche Lilies that matched her wreath, along with a few of the palest pink wildflowers.

At last it was time for the ceremony to begin. Furry-Ball and Sunshine began the music, and to Faith's embarrassment, their whistling took on a very loud and lively form, and sometimes it was even off-key. She motioned to them to slow down, and even put her finger to her mouth, but they were so intent in their whistling that they did not see her. For all of her embarrassment, however, the bandits seemed to thoroughly enjoy it. In fact, some even clapped!

A hush came over the crowd as Tidy-Paw and Aunt Serenity took their places, and the music at last began to slow down. And then everyone grew quieter still as the ceremony began.

Waddler stepped out in front with Seeker and Truster. A single white lily was tucked into his fur, and his eyes searched the crowd for his bride. Posie stood shyly, ready to be escorted down the pathway by Puddly and Trasher. For a minute, their eyes met. It was a look that would last a lifetime for both of them, and as is the case with love, only they could translate it.

The wedding march began. Much to Faith's relief, it was slower and more quiet this time, lending a much more dignified air to what was happening. (And though she felt the music was much more appropriate, if you had been there, you might not have agreed, because you would have recognized the tune as "The Battle Hymn of the Republic"!)

Joy stepped out and started down the path, scattering flowers from her bouquet in great abundance along the way. Faith followed, beaming with happiness.

It would be hard to say what went through Posie's mind right before she walked down the pathway because many thoughts came to her. She thought of her family and friends. How grateful she felt for each of them! And then she thought of Waddler. How good The Maker was to give her a husband like him!

But it would be only fair to say that she did have one fleeting moment of sadness. She thought of Methuselah and how she wished that he were there this day. Then as quickly as the thought had come, another replaced it—the realization that he was there in a sense. All that was in his heart, all that he had taught them, and even all for whom he cared were there.

"Thank You, Dear Maker, for this wonderful thought," she whispered.

She stepped forward, escorted by her brothers, a bit timidly, but never losing sight of Waddler, whose adoring eyes were fixed on her. She was smiling (and blushing ever so slightly) under her veil.

But while all of this was happening, something else of equal importance was taking place. The bandits who had come, some out of curiosity, others under duress, had totally forgotten their reasons for coming. Instead, they were overwhelmed with the beauty of the ceremony. But even more, they were struck with the force of the lives of those who followed The Maker. They realized that each of these whom they had mocked and from whom they had stolen treated them with respect and even love. Not only had they helped them to find food and shelter, they had also cared for their sick and dying. These were, in truth, their friends, and they felt very unworthy and ashamed of their words and actions. All of this, combined with the simple beauty of the two who were being married, caused more than one of them to wipe away a tear.

It was to them, as well as to Posie and Waddler, that Seeker preached the wedding sermon. He did not mince words, nor did he scold the bandits for their bad deeds. He simply preached about The Maker. He told them that The Maker had created them and their forest. He said that once they had been friends with The Maker, but that they had turned against Him. He even reminded them that once they had been friends with the Uprights. At this, the bandits looked at one another with knowing glances. They had heard rumors of this from time to time. However, Seeker's next remark really shocked them.

"It may surprise you to know that not all Uprights are Upright." He explained further. "Of course, once they were. But when they broke faith with The Maker, they were no longer Upright. They only looked Upright. But The Maker does not only look at the outside. He looks at the heart." The bandits leaned forward. They were confused.

"Of course, some Uprights *are* Upright. But all too many are not." The bandits nodded in agreement—they were beginning to understand. "It's having your heart made clean that makes you truly Upright—not walking on only two feet. And The Maker alone can do the cleaning. You see, while they and we deserved to die for turning against The Maker, He died in our place. Now all that's left to do is turn to Him and take the masks off our hearts and let Him make us clean and Upright." The bandits did not move a muscle. They were thinking about what he said, and they knew it to be true in the deepest part of their hearts.

Then he continued. "Everyone here remembers Methuselah." They nodded. "There wasn't a more Upright raccoon in the whole forest. Why, even his death saved a life." Everyone looked over at Rapid. They remembered very well. They also remembered that they had left Rapid to die.

Seeker opened The Book and read, " 'The generation of the Upright will be blessed.' " He looked out at them and then at Waddler and Posie. "We are here today to celebrate that fact— that Waddler and Posie stand before us today because of their belief in The Maker. And where did they get it? From Methuselah—from his teaching and his example. And where did that come from? The Book. And where did The Book come from? The Maker Himself. And in the same way, you, too, can be blessed by Him." The bandits looked very thoughtful at this part of the sermon.

"Friends, we are watching a blessing right before our very eyes. It is a great happiness that Waddler and Posie are joining their lives this day. Think about their lives for a moment. Many of you have been blessed because of their help. You see, there are no disadvantages in following The Maker—only advantages."

It was true. The bandits looked at themselves—scarred, thin, mangy, and most of all, unhappy. Then they looked at Waddler and Posie. Though Waddler no longer had his beautiful tail, his face shone, and so did Posie's. That was what the bandits noticed—a radiance that almost made Waddler and Posie seem transparent with nothing to hide. The bandits thought of themselves again. They had many things they wished they could hide— stealing, greed, violence, and most of all, a feeling of worthlessness, as if they really didn't even deserve to be alive. All they had ever done in life was to take. And they were more ashamed than ever. In fact, their shame made them want more than anything else to be made Upright.

Seeker was speaking again. "What The Maker did for Methuselah and Posie and Waddler and many more of us, He can do for you. If you would like to be Upright in heart, bow your head to The Maker and ask Him to remove your mask and make you His follower." Together, they prayed. And when they looked up, many had done just that. In fact, it made such an impression on them that one by one, they stood in an Upright position to demonstrate what had happened in their hearts. Seeker looked out at them, and he rejoiced to see their belief shown so clearly.

"The Maker be praised!" he said, and quietly, they all sat down.

Then Seeker asked Posie and Waddler to say their vows.

Posie turned to Waddler, smiling demurely, "I, Posie, promise to be your faithful wife, but always putting The Maker first. And I will love you and serve you whether you are sick or well, as long as The Maker gives me life."

Waddler looked at Posie tenderly. "And I, Waddler, promise to love you—second only to The Maker—with all my heart. And

I will protect you with my life and give my life to you freely, as long as The Maker gives me life."

Seeker prayed. He prayed that The Maker would not only bless their life together, as He had promised, but that the gift of belief in The Maker would be passed on to their children and many others.

Then Seeker cleared his throat. "And now, Waddler may kiss the bride."

The bandits leaned forward with great interest. But Furry-Ball did not watch. He covered his eyes—at least he seemed to. (In reality, he peeked. Though later, when accused by Sunshine, he said that he needed to be ready to start the wedding recessional on time, and that is why he peeked.)

And the recessional was not only on time, but loud and fast too. To Sarah, sitting high above in the tree, it seemed like a beautiful medley of "The Star Spangled Banner" and "The Hallelujah Chorus," with just a tinge of "Yankee Doodle."

And then it was time for the festivities. Such singing and games had never taken place in the forest before with all of the bandits getting along with one another and laughing together. The cake was distributed fairly by Furry-Ball and Sunshine, who made sure that no one took two pieces! And then it was time for all to wish the bride and groom The Maker's blessing. As each one came through the receiving line, it was surprising how many told Waddler and Posie that this very day they had become followers of The Maker. Those remarks were like wedding gifts to them, and they remembered them for a long time.

There was another special gift, too—the Upright mover. The family had decorated it with flowers, and Furry-Ball had made a sign especially for the occasion. It read: JUST MERRIED.

Waddler and Posie were to leave that very night for their new home far away. They were going back to the foreign country where Waddler and Trasher had already begun their work.

As the family gathered around to say their good-byes, Seeker read from The Book. "The Lord knows the days of the Upright, and their inheritance shall be forever."

"The Maker go with you!" they shouted together.

And some distance away, having quietly climbed down from her hiding place in the tree, with tears filling her eyes, Sarah waved her own farewell.

Posie waved back, and her eyes, too, filled with tears at the memories of her friendship with Sarah. They had shared so much together. She thought of how Sarah had given her those first apples, and then the most precious gift—The Book. But most of all they shared a love for Methuselah and The Maker. Posie would miss her dear friend. She waved one last time.

Though the past would never be forgotten, her new life with Waddler was about to begin. As Posie held on tightly behind, Waddler gave the mover a push, and they sped forward down the hill and disappeared into the forest—but not before Waddler turned to give his bride a kiss. And this time, Furry-Ball did not cover his eyes!

Posie would miss her dear friend. She waved one last time.

About the Author

Mary Elizabeth Edgren, a grandmother of three, enjoys telling stories to children. Especially stories about animals. Each Sunday morning, a group of little people gathers around her at the Fort Lewis Chapel for the children's sermon, a biblical lesson often illustrated with a vignette from the animal kingdom. Wild creatures are no strangers to the Edgren home, with daily visits by raccoons, opossums, squirrels, jays, myriad other creatures, and an occasional fox. A sequel to *Methuselah's Gift, Methuselah's Heart* continues the adventures of a delightful, and very human, raccoon family.